WHEN VEGETABLES ATTACK

by Mark Burgess
illustrated by Bridget MacKeith

Librarian Reviewer
Chris Kreie
Media Specialist, Eden Prairie Schools, MN
M.S. in Information Media, St. Cloud State University, MN

Reading Consultant
Elizabeth Stedem
Educator/Consultant, Colorado Springs, CO
MA in Elementary Education, University of Denver, CO

STONE ARCH BOOKS
Minneapolis San Diego

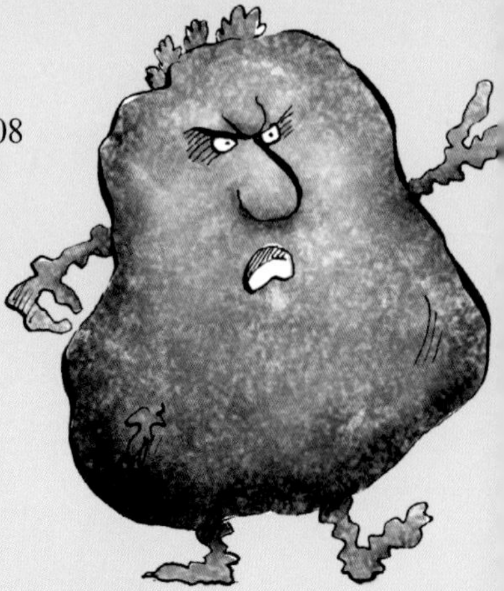

First published in the United States in 2008
by Stone Arch Books
151 Good Counsel Drive, P.O. Box 669
Mankato, Minnesota 56002
www.stonearchbooks.com

Originally published in Great Britain in 2003
by A & C Black Publishers Ltd
38 Soho Square, London, W1D 3HB

Library of Congress Cataloging-in-Publication Data
Burgess, Mark.
[Agent Spike and the Vegetables of Doom]
When Vegetables Attack / by Mark Burgess; illustrated by Bridget MacKeith.
p. cm. — (Graphic Trax)
Originally published: Agent Spike and the Vegetables of Doom. London: A. & C. Black, 2003.
ISBN 978-1-4342-0458-5 (library binding)
ISBN 978-1-4342-0508-7 (paperback)
1. Graphic novels. I. MacKeith, Bridget. II. Title.
PN6737.B87A34 2008
741.5'941—dc22 2007030802

Summary: When a science experiment goes terribly wrong, a group of mutant veggies threatens to take over the world! Luckily, Agent Spike of the Secret Service is on the case. With help from a few tomatoes, Spike tries to stop this produce posse and their leader, the Big Pumpkin.

Art Director: Heather Kindseth
Graphic Designer: Brann Garvey
Colorist: Keila Ramos

1 2 3 4 5 6 13 12 11 10 09 08

Printed in the United States of America

TABLE OF CONTENTS

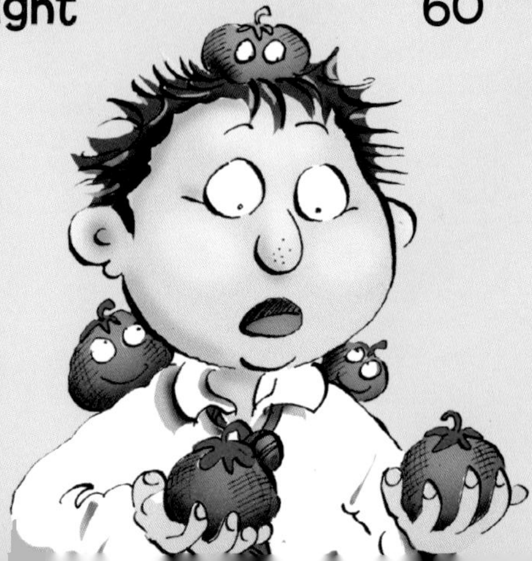

Cast of Characters

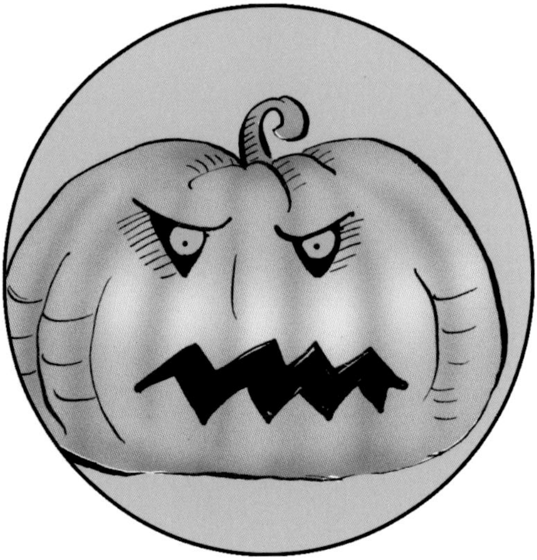

The Big Pumpkin

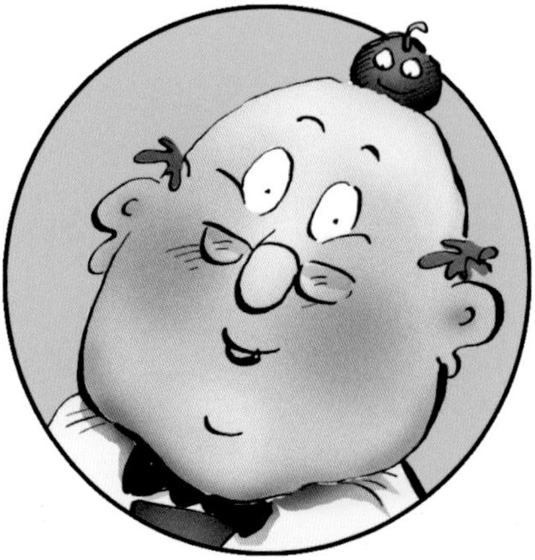

The Professor

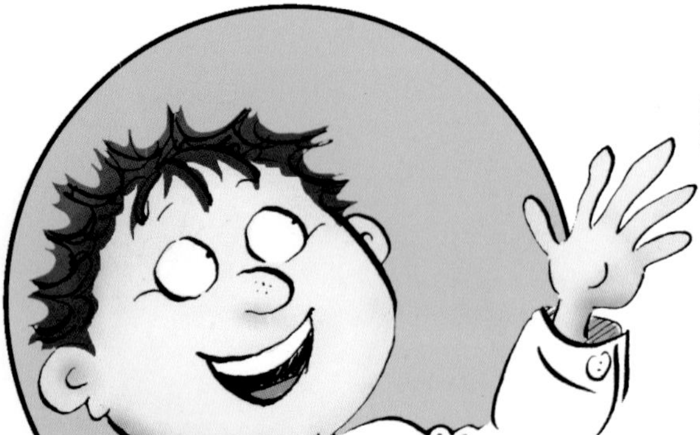

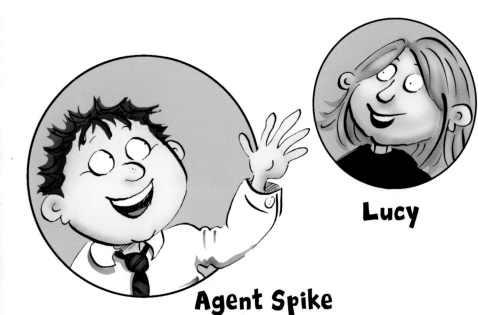

Agent Spike

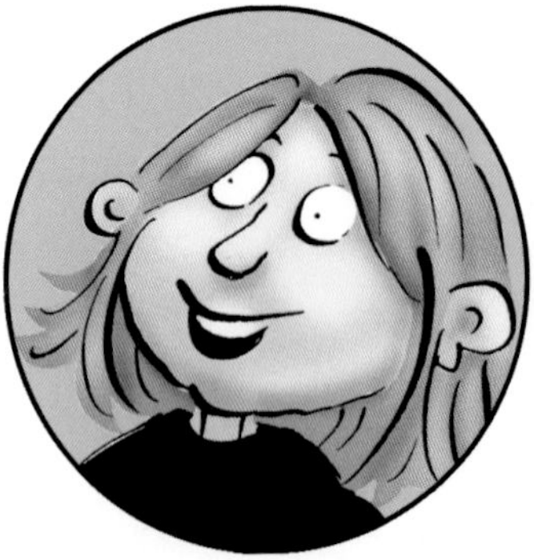

Lucy

Chapter One

One day at school, Spike was hard at work. Suddenly, the screen in front of him flickered. The Director of the Secret Service appeared on the screen. This could only mean one thing: an urgent job for Agent Spike.

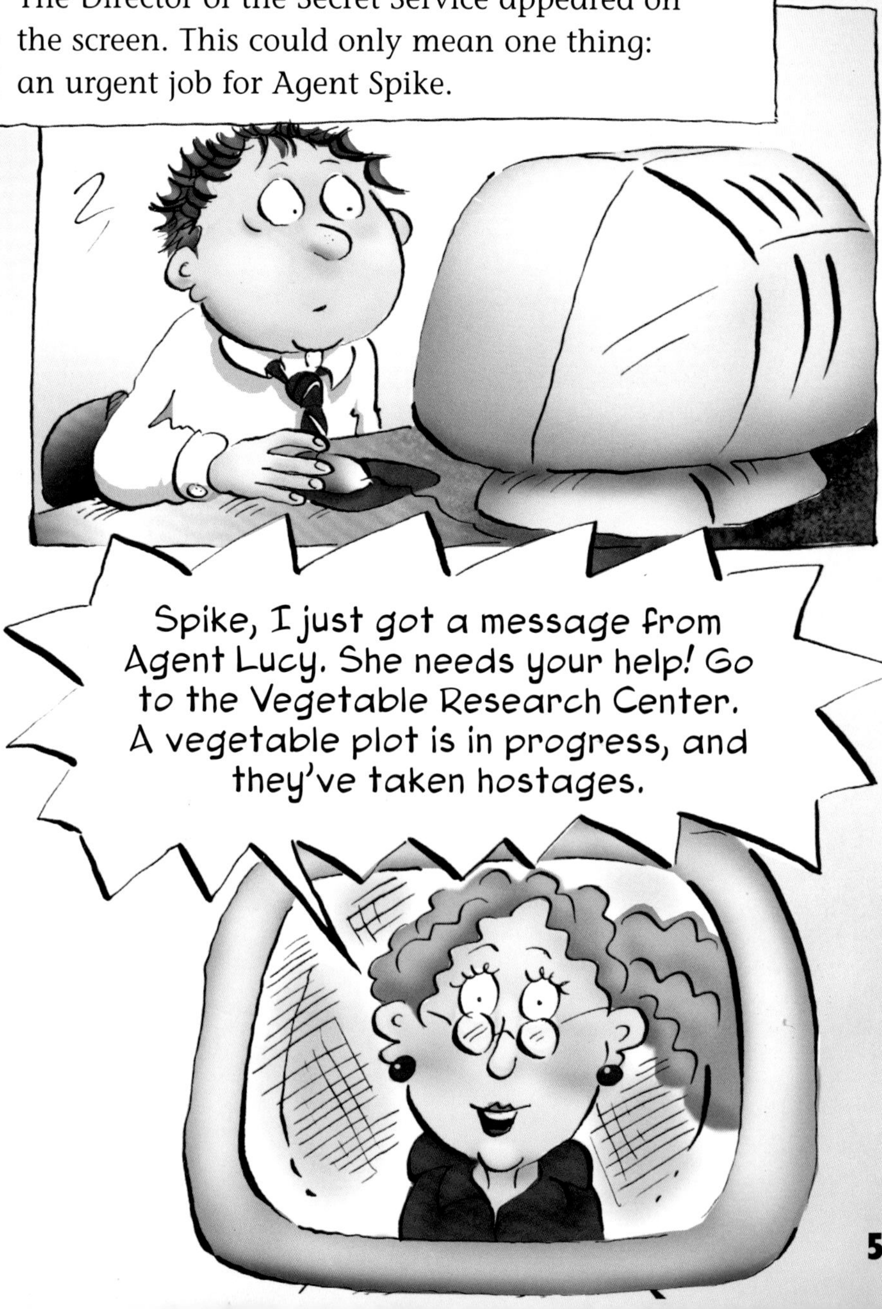
Spike, I just got a message from Agent Lucy. She needs your help! Go to the Vegetable Research Center. A vegetable plot is in progress, and they've taken hostages.

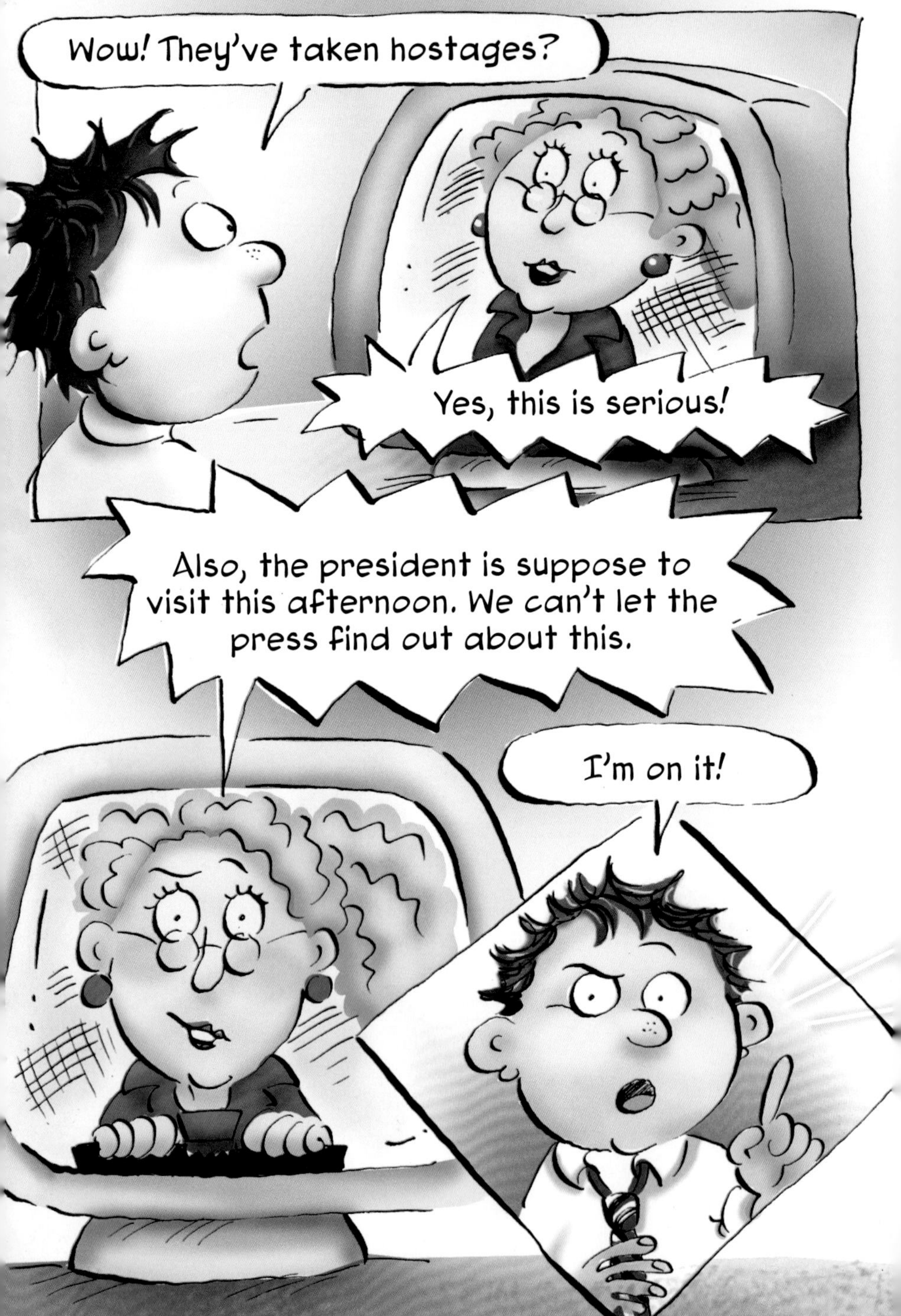
Wow! They've taken hostages?
Yes, this is serious!
Also, the president is suppose to visit this afternoon. We can't let the press find out about this.
I'm on it!

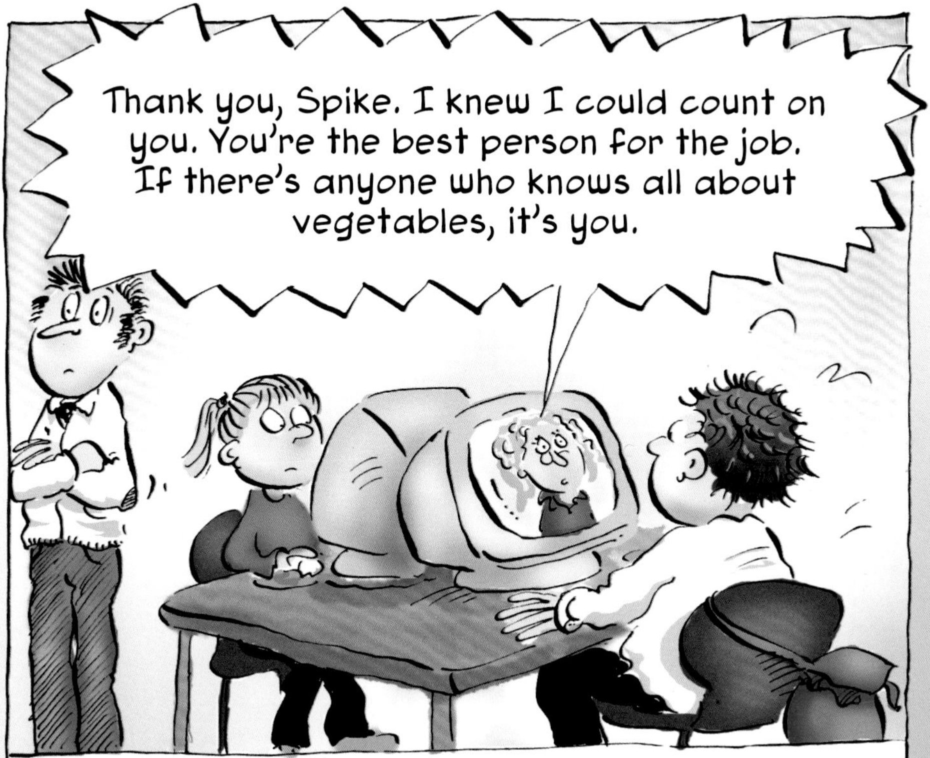
Thank you, Spike. I knew I could count on you. You're the best person for the job. If there's anyone who knows all about vegetables, it's you.

The director was right. Spike was great at growing things.

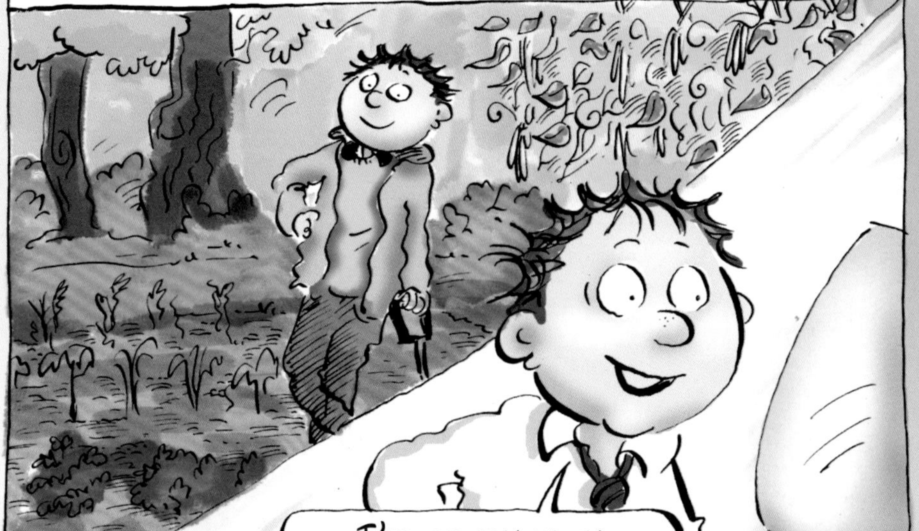
I'm on my way.

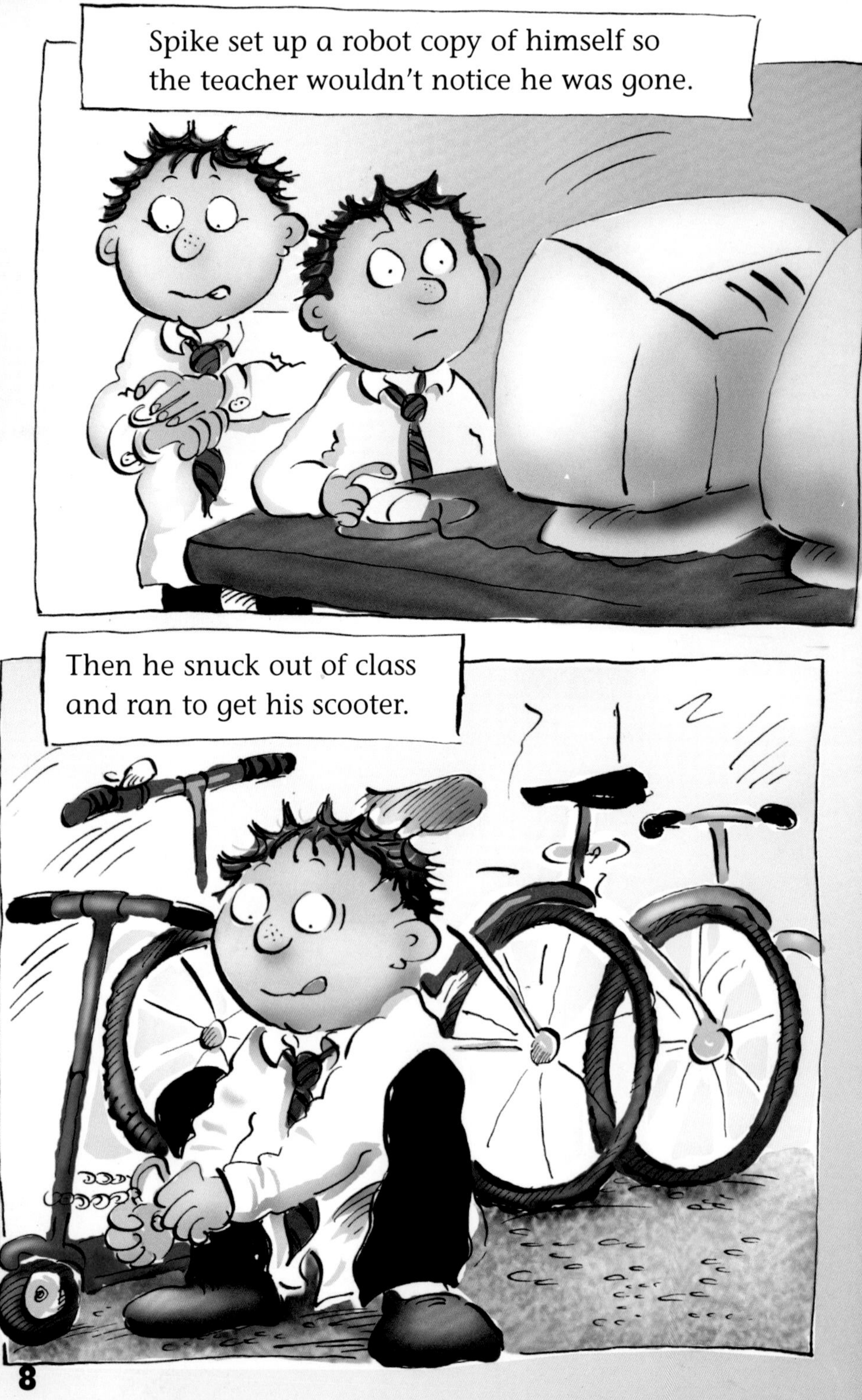
Spike set up a robot copy of himself so the teacher wouldn't notice he was gone.
Then he snuck out of class and ran to get his scooter.

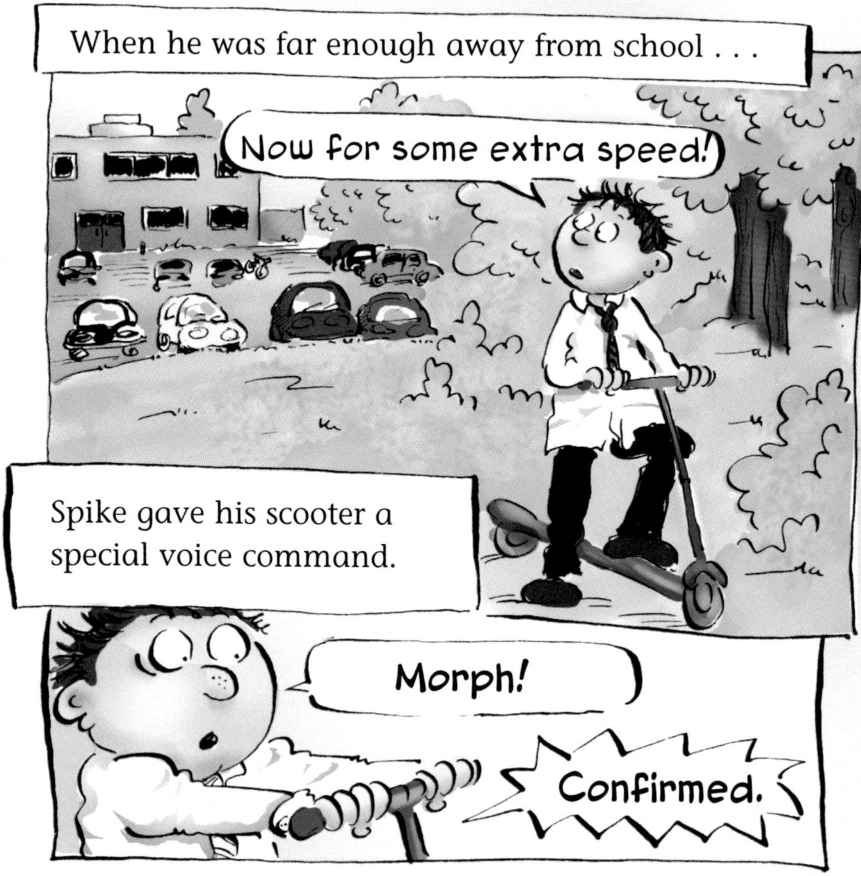
When he was far enough away from school . . .
Now for some extra speed!
Spike gave his scooter a special voice command.
Morph!
Confirmed.

Instantly, Spike's scooter changed into a race car.

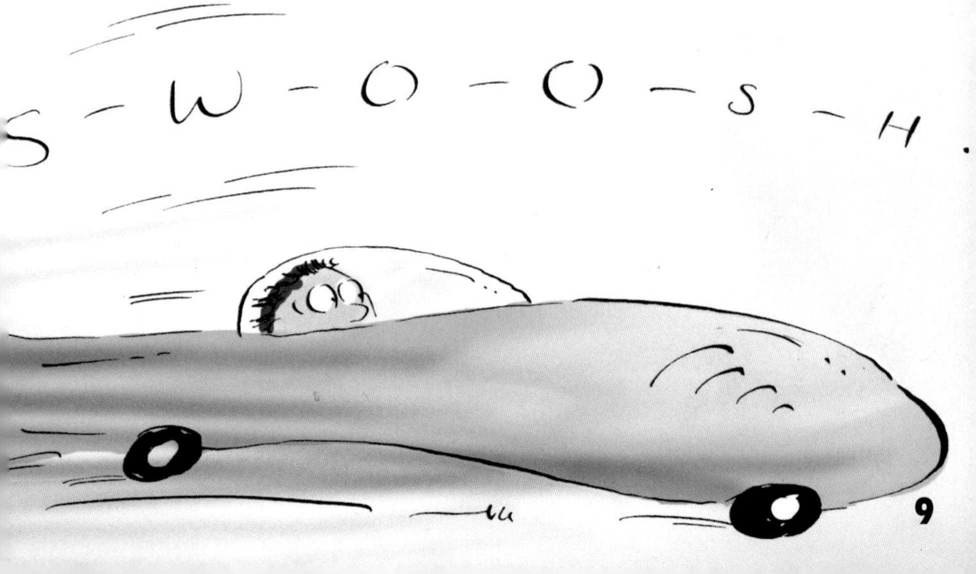
S-W-O-O-S-H.

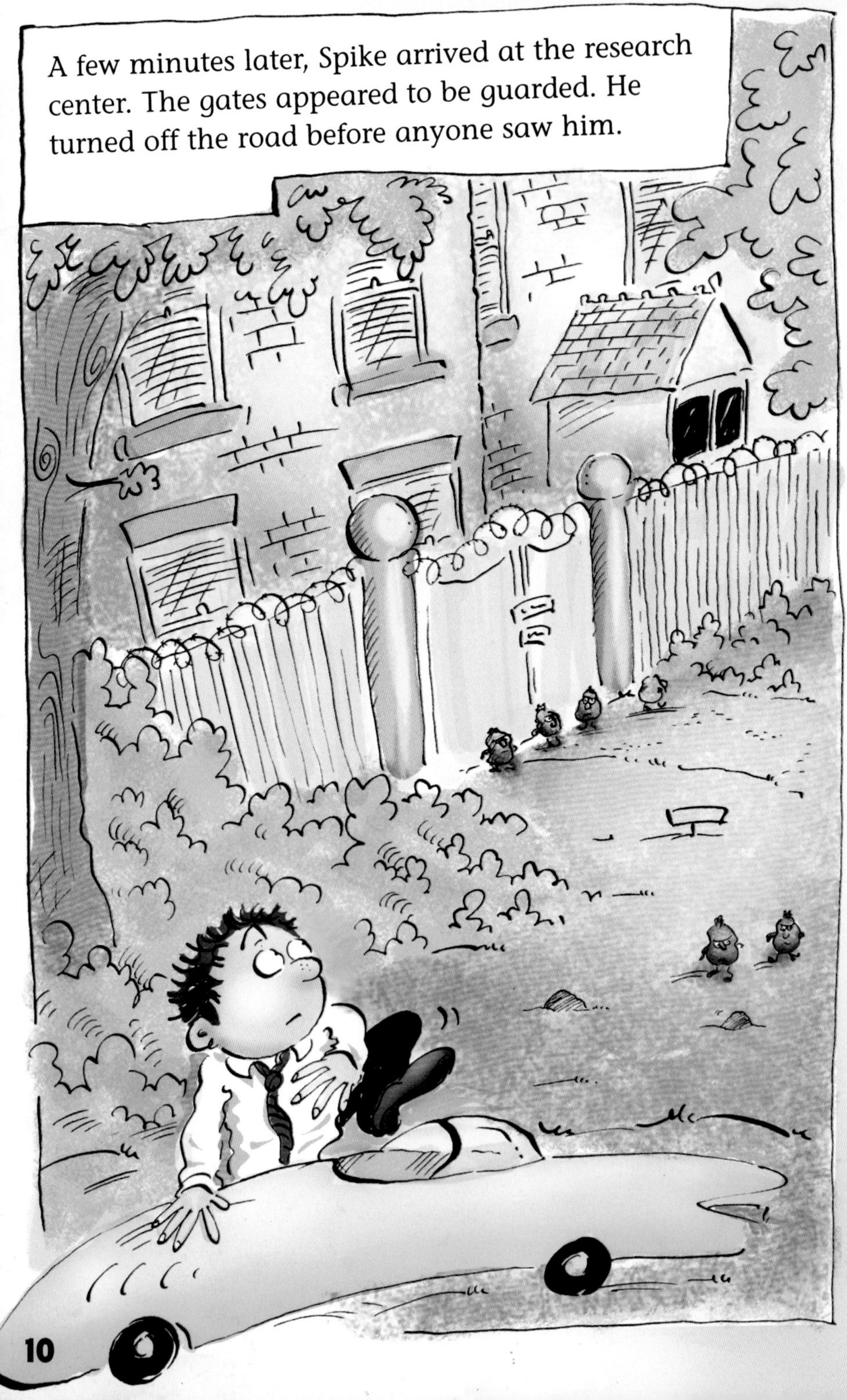
A few minutes later, Spike arrived at the research center. The gates appeared to be guarded. He turned off the road before anyone saw him.

Chapter Two

Spike hid his race car in the bushes and crept closer. There were guards everywhere.

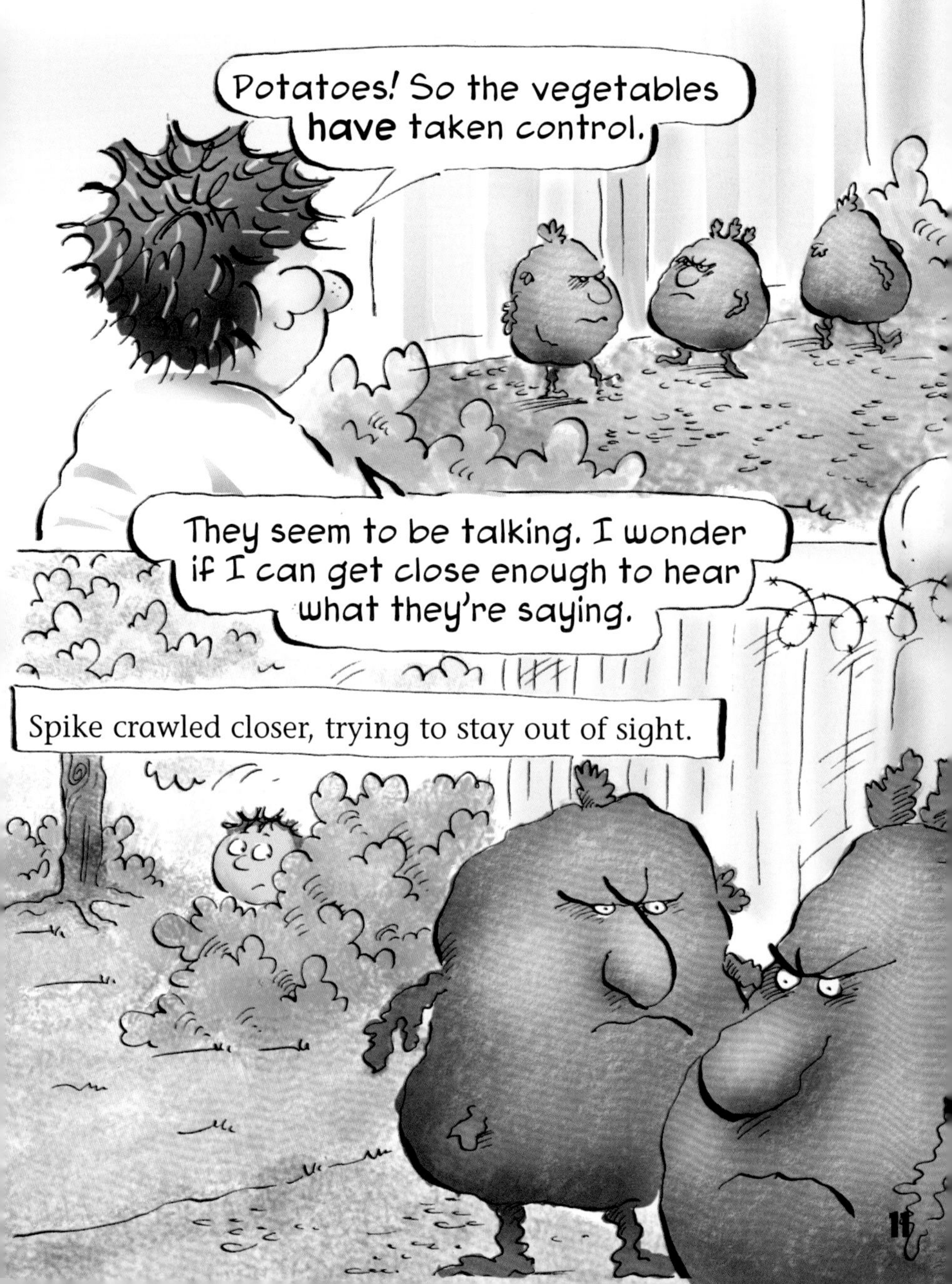

Potatoes! So the vegetables **have** taken control.
They seem to be talking. I wonder if I can get close enough to hear what they're saying.
Spike crawled closer, trying to stay out of sight.

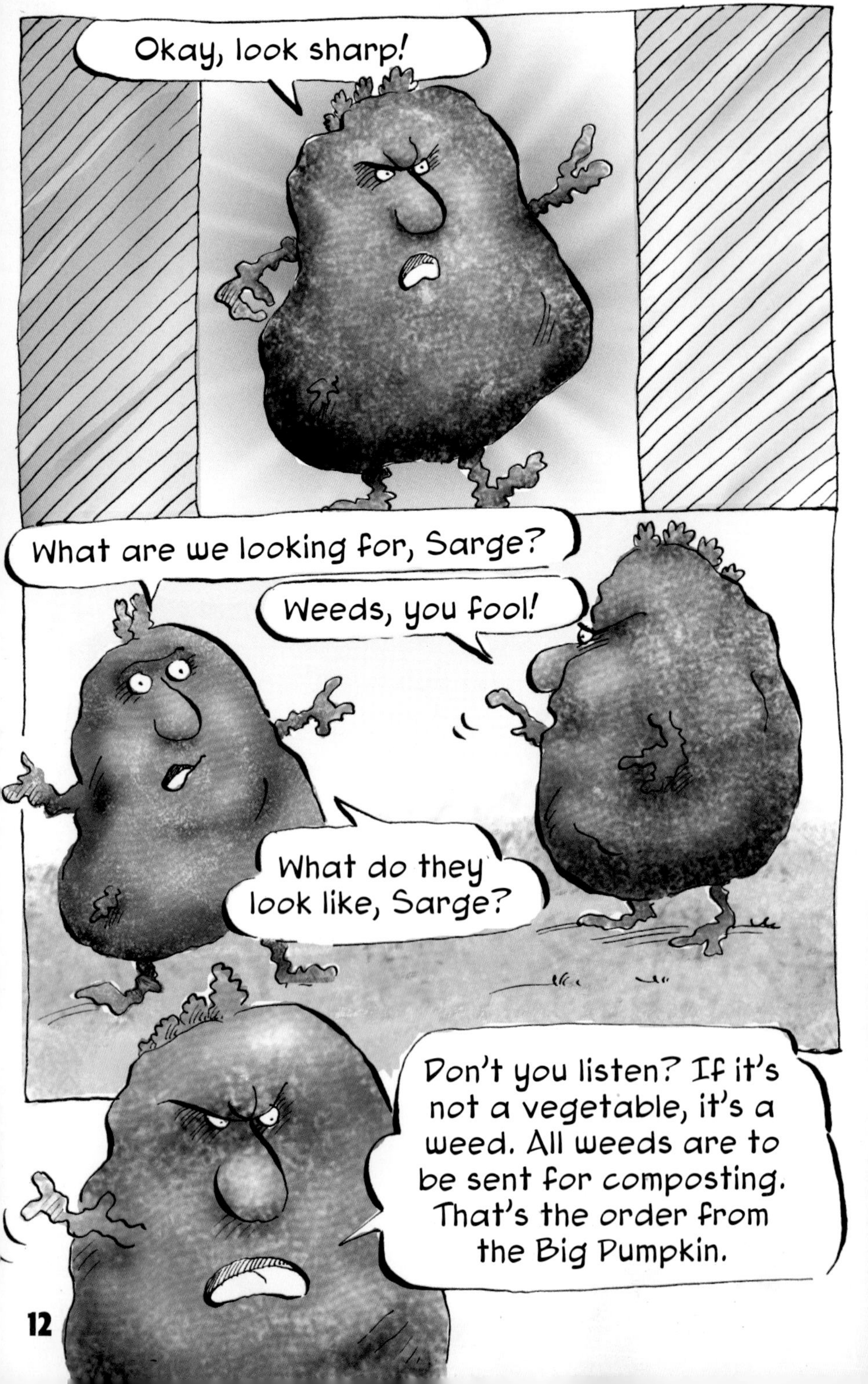
Okay, look sharp!
What are we looking for, Sarge?
Weeds, you fool!
What do they look like, Sarge?
Don't you listen? If it's not a vegetable, it's a weed. All weeds are to be sent for composting. That's the order from the Big Pumpkin.

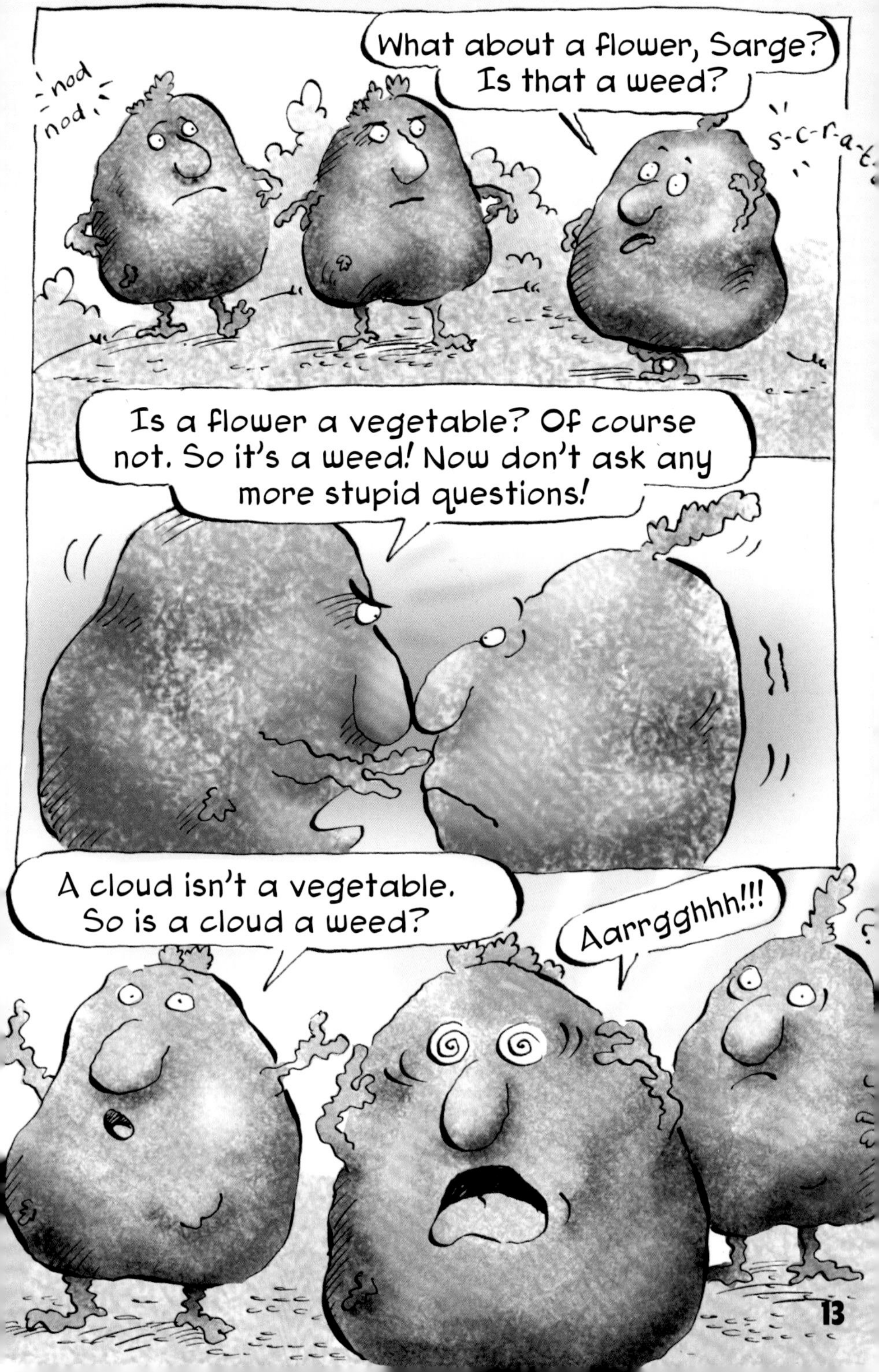
nod
nod
What about a flower, Sarge?
Is that a weed?
s-c-r-a-t
Is a flower a vegetable? Of course not. So it's a weed! Now don't ask any more stupid questions!
A cloud isn't a vegetable.
So is a cloud a weed?
Aarrgghhh!!!

Oh, no! The vegetables have minds of their own. This might be bad for humans. The veggies will be angry at us for eating them. I better watch out. I don't want to be composted!

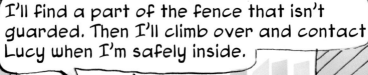

Spike crept away underneath the bushes.

I'll find a part of the fence that isn't guarded. Then I'll climb over and contact Lucy when I'm safely inside.

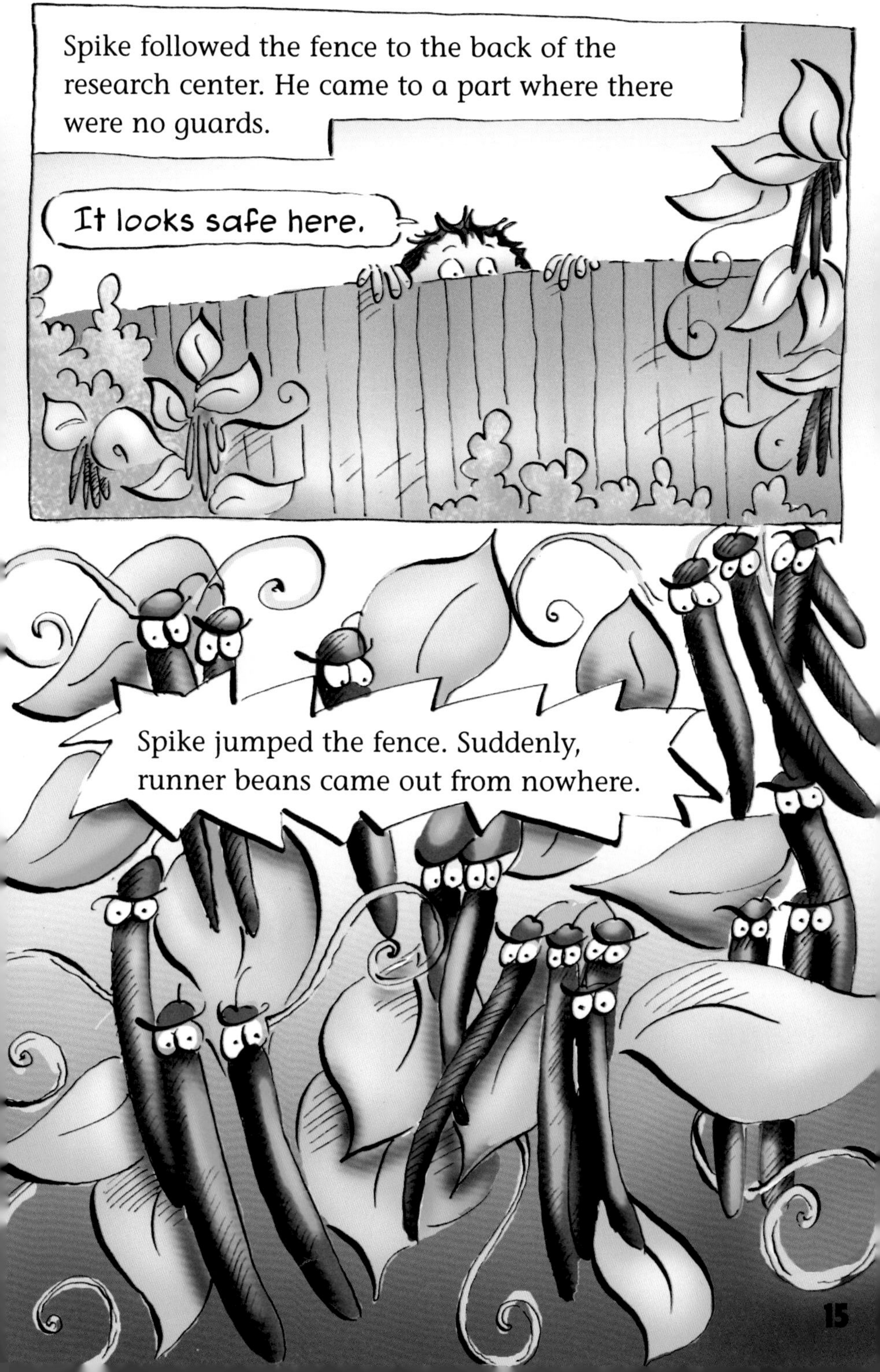
Spike followed the fence to the back of the research center. He came to a part where there were no guards.
It looks safe here.
Spike jumped the fence. Suddenly, runner beans came out from nowhere.

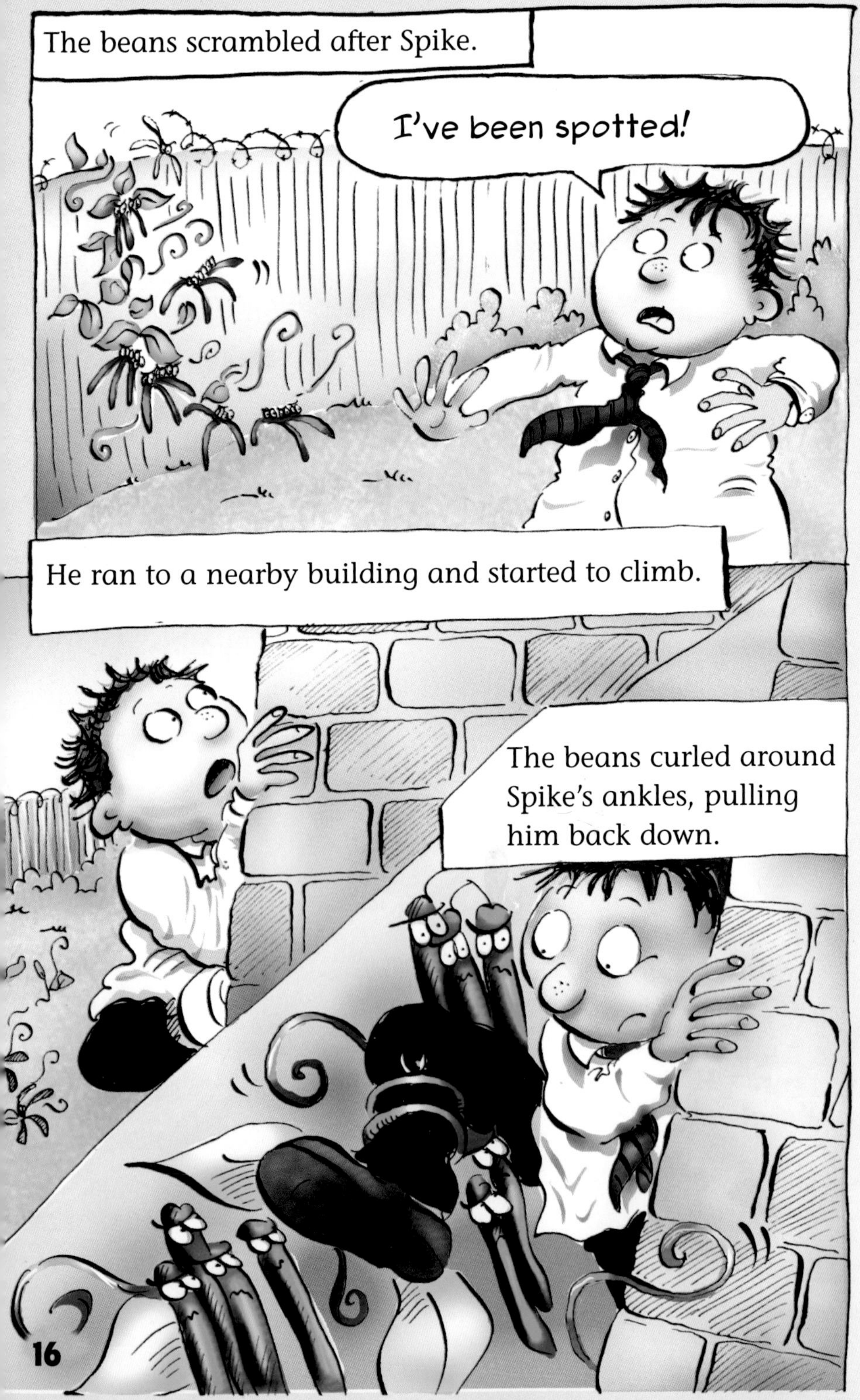
The beans scrambled after Spike.
I've been spotted!
He ran to a nearby building and started to climb.
The beans curled around Spike's ankles, pulling him back down.

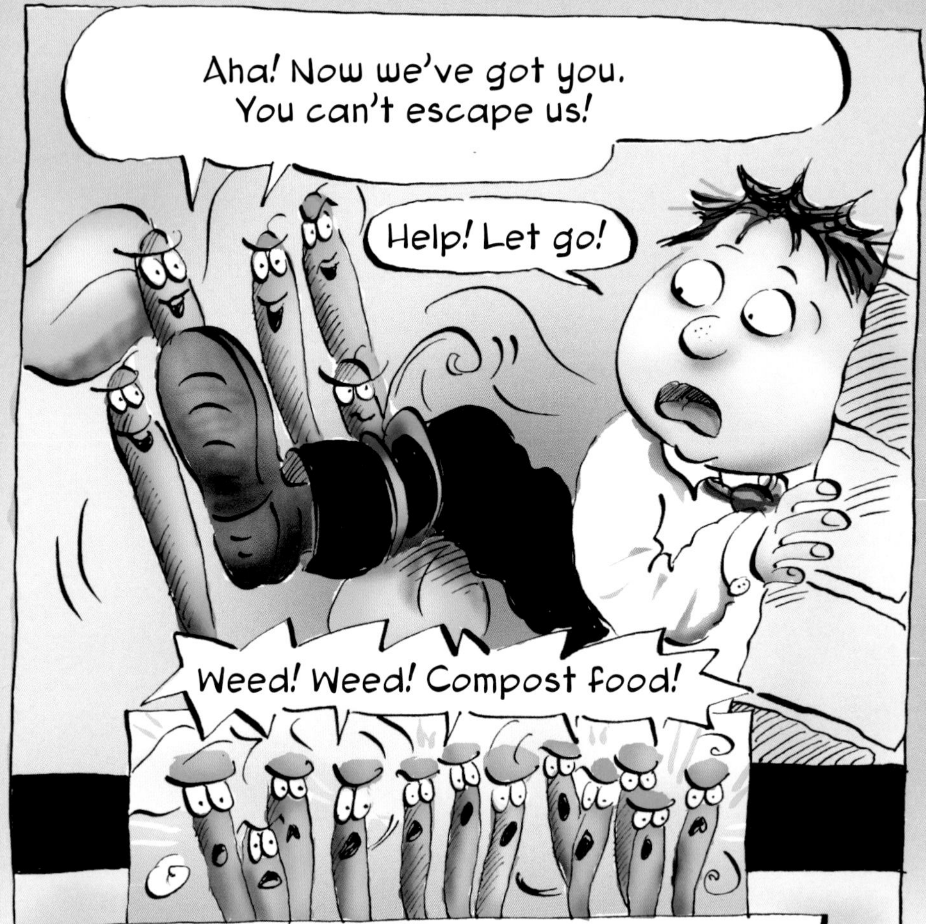
Aha! Now we've got you.
You can't escape us!
Help! Let go!
Weed! Weed! Compost food!

Spike struggled hard, but the beans held on tighter and tighter.

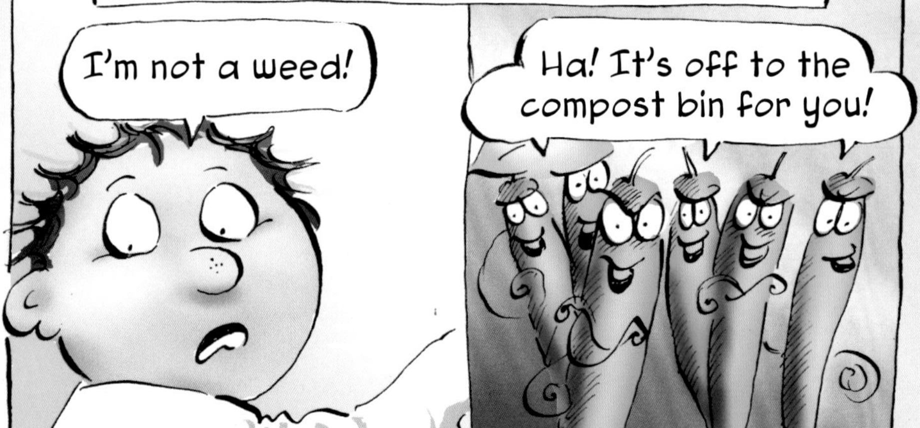
I'm not a weed!
Ha! It's off to the compost bin for you!

Chapter Three

The runner beans were pulling hard, and Spike was starting to slip off the wall. Then he had an idea.

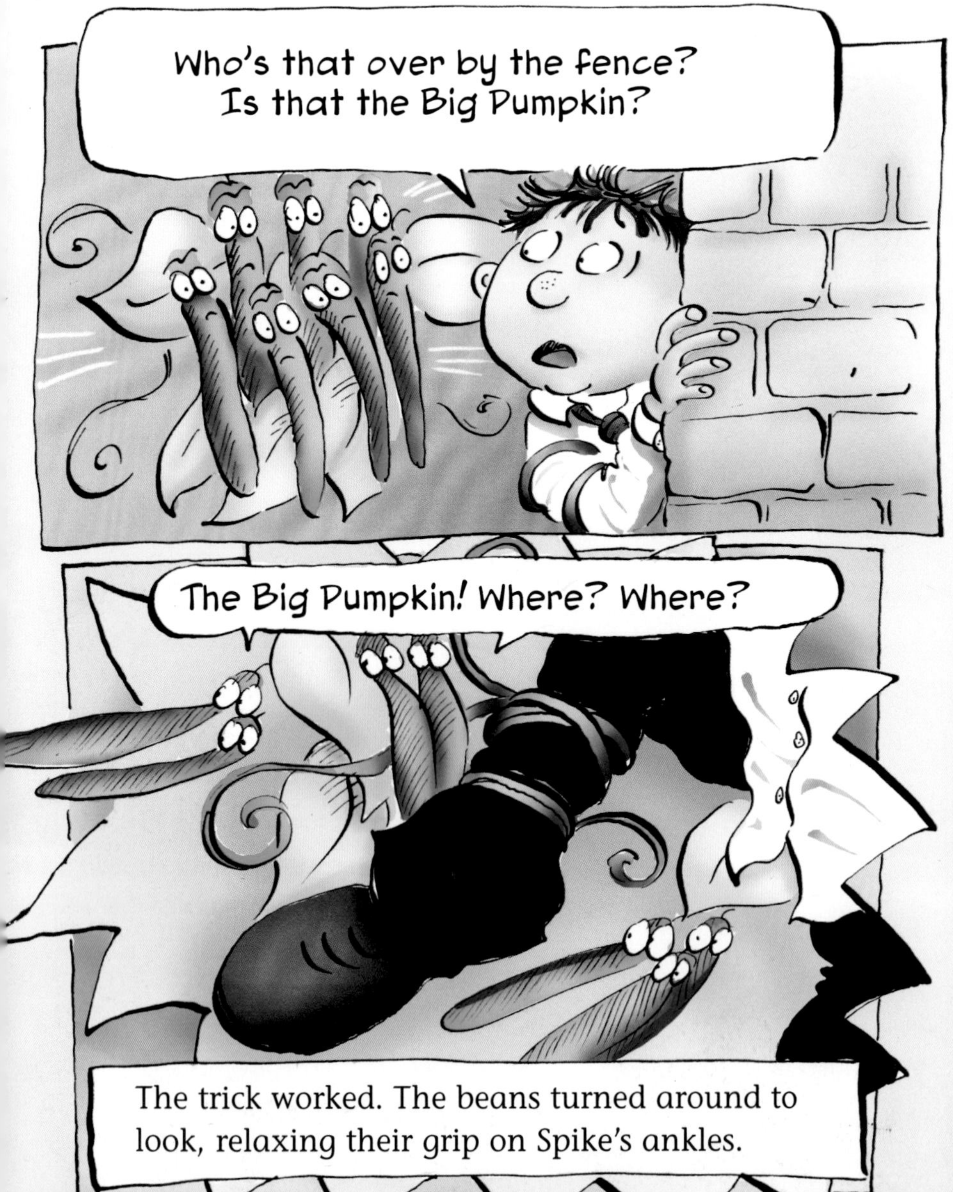

Who's that over by the fence?
Is that the Big Pumpkin?
The Big Pumpkin! Where? Where?

The trick worked. The beans turned around to look, relaxing their grip on Spike's ankles.

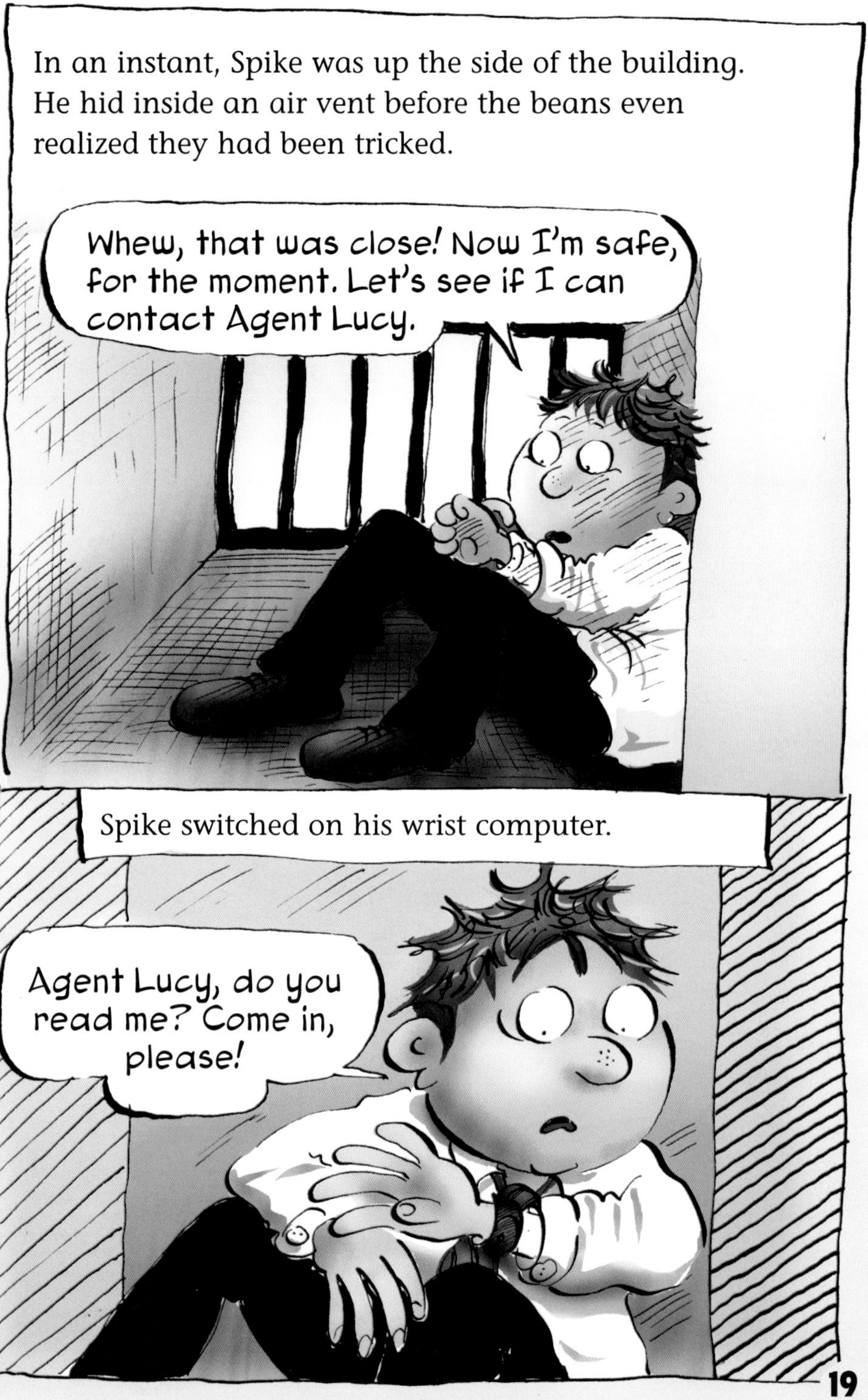
In an instant, Spike was up the side of the building. He hid inside an air vent before the beans even realized they had been tricked.
Whew, that was close! Now I'm safe, for the moment. Let's see if I can contact Agent Lucy.
Spike switched on his wrist computer.
Agent Lucy, do you read me? Come in, please!

Agent Lucy appeared on the screen. She looked like she was in trouble. Strange red blobs were swarming all over her.

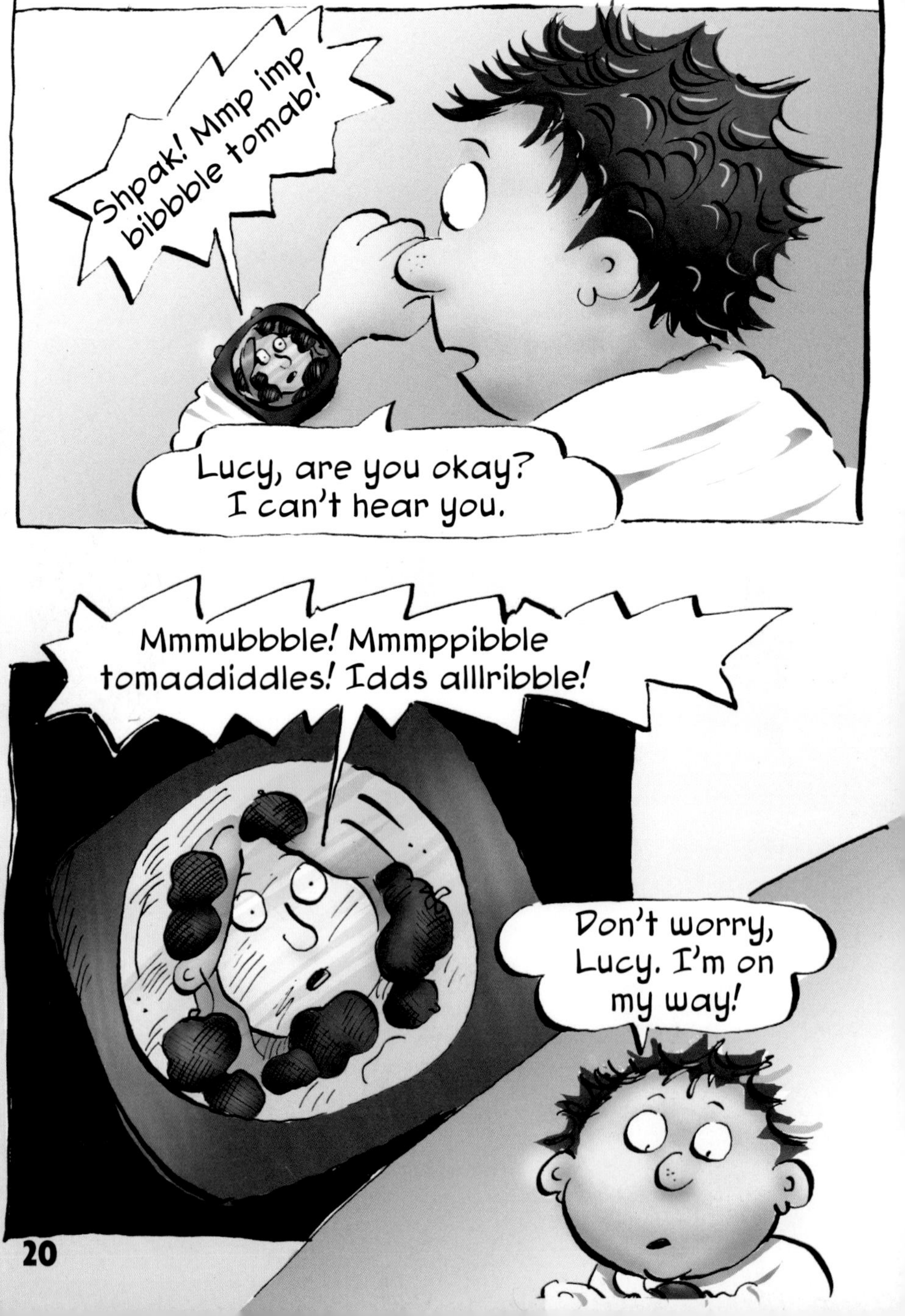
Shpak! Mmp imp bibbble tomab!
Lucy, are you okay? I can't hear you.
Mmmubbble! Mmmppibble tomaddiddles! Idds alllribble!
Don't worry, Lucy. I'm on my way!

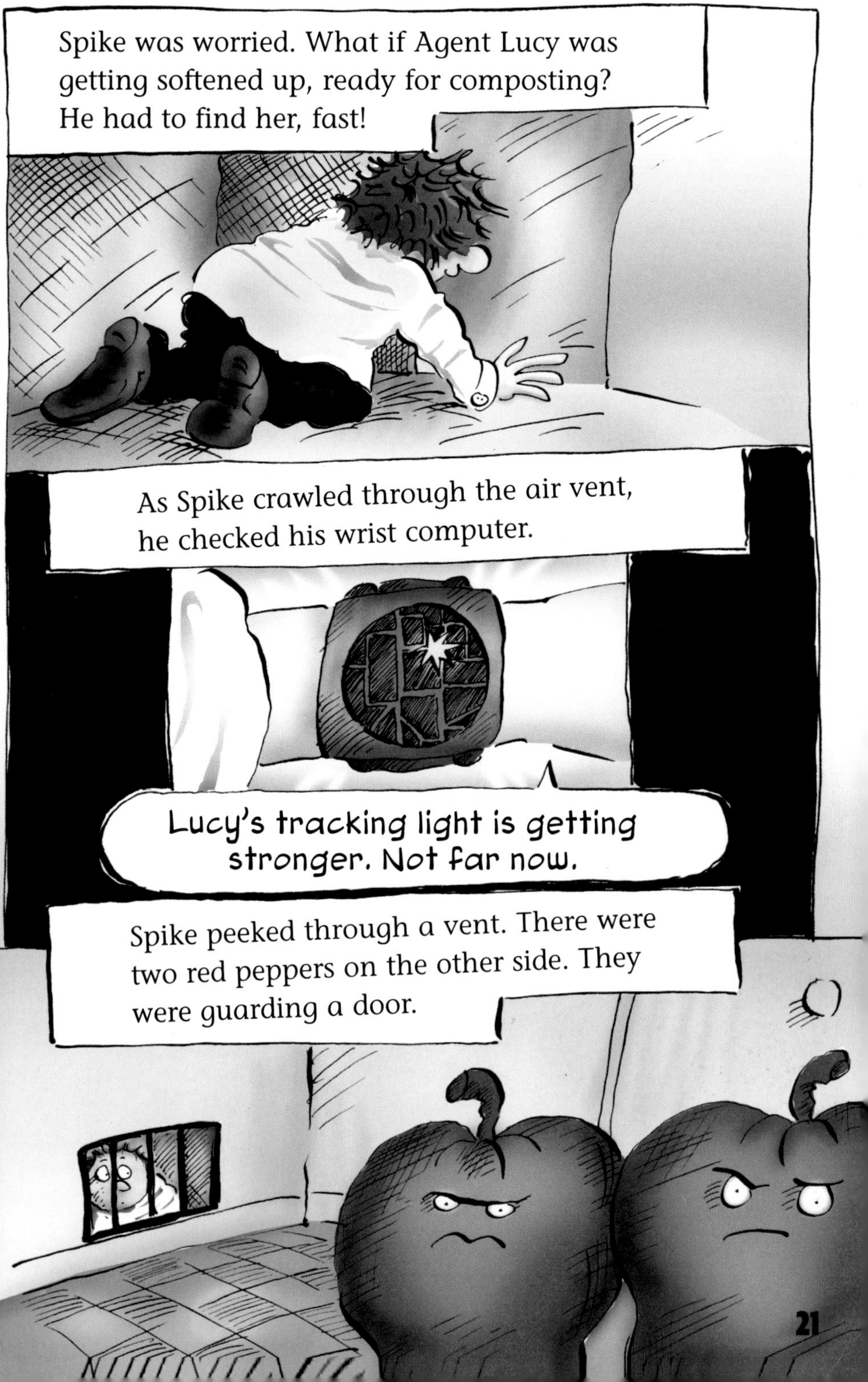
Spike was worried. What if Agent Lucy was getting softened up, ready for composting? He had to find her, fast!
As Spike crawled through the air vent, he checked his wrist computer.
Lucy's tracking light is getting stronger. Not far now.
Spike peeked through a vent. There were two red peppers on the other side. They were guarding a door.

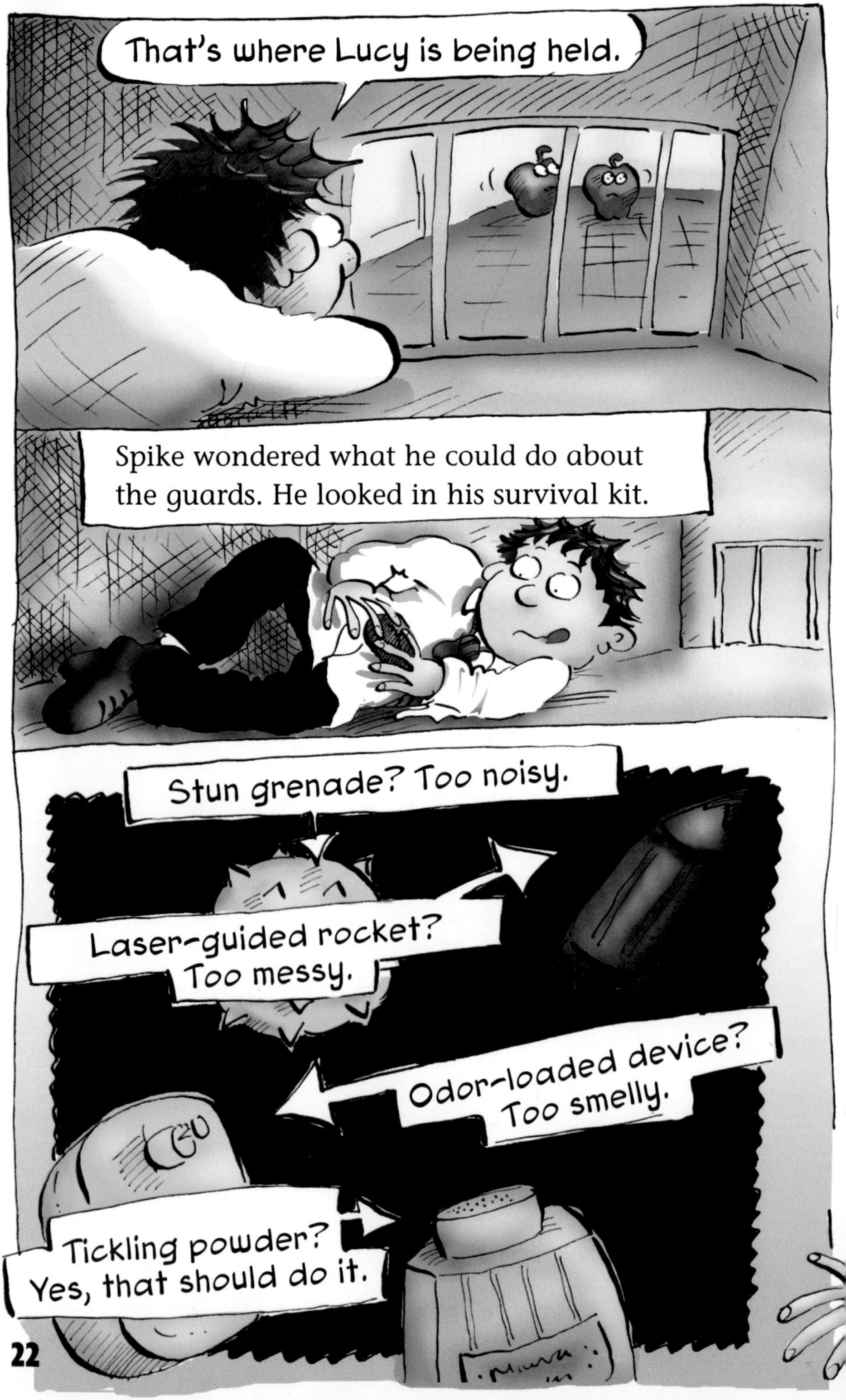
That's where Lucy is being held.
Spike wondered what he could do about the guards. He looked in his survival kit.
Stun grenade? Too noisy.
Laser-guided rocket? Too messy.
Odor-loaded device? Too smelly.
Tickling powder? Yes, that should do it.

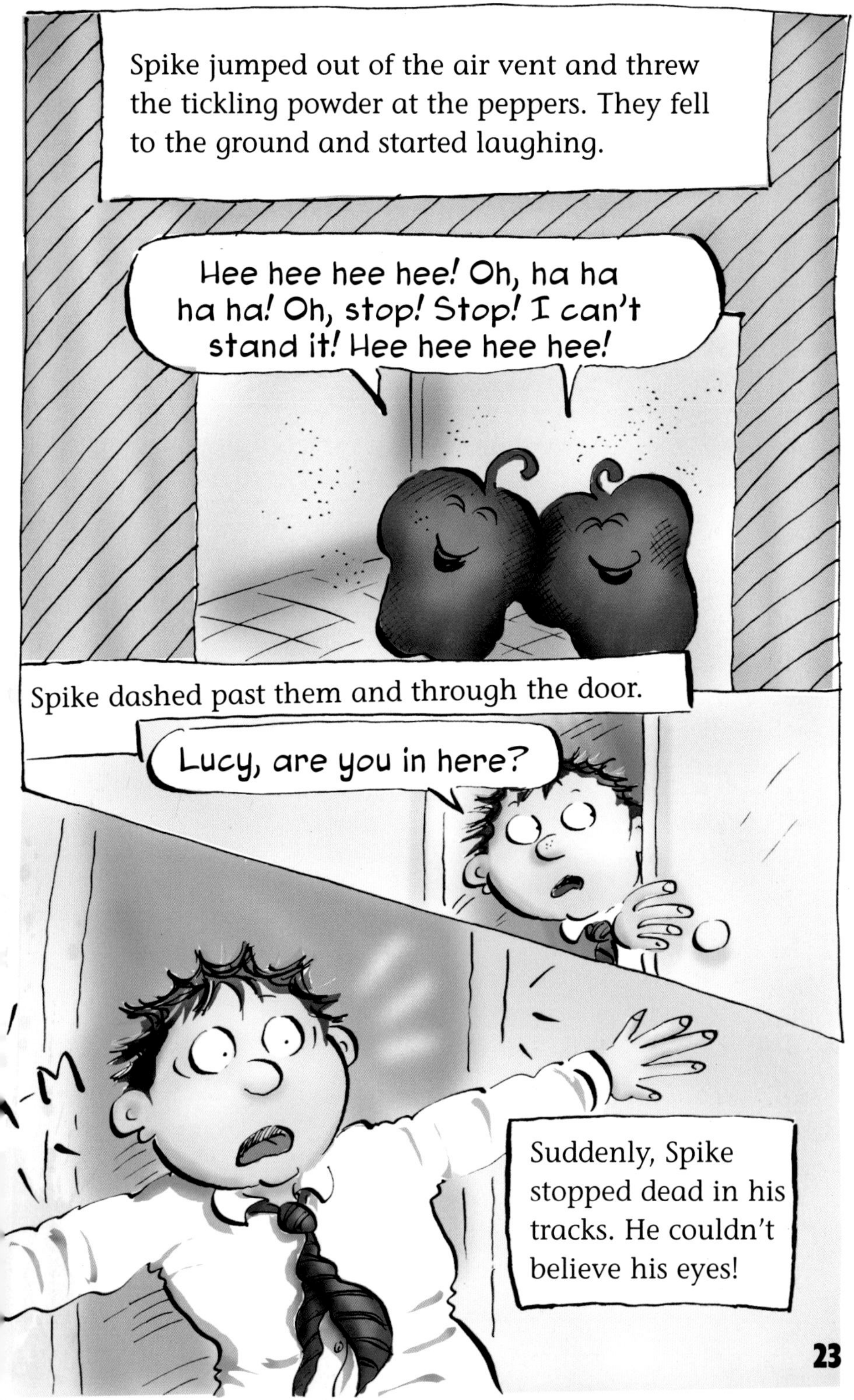
Spike jumped out of the air vent and threw the tickling powder at the peppers. They fell to the ground and started laughing.
Hee hee hee hee! Oh, ha ha ha ha! Oh, stop! Stop! I can't stand it! Hee hee hee hee!
Spike dashed past them and through the door.
Lucy, are you in here?
Suddenly, Spike stopped dead in his tracks. He couldn't believe his eyes!

Chapter Four

A swarm of red blobs came from nowhere and jumped all over Spike!

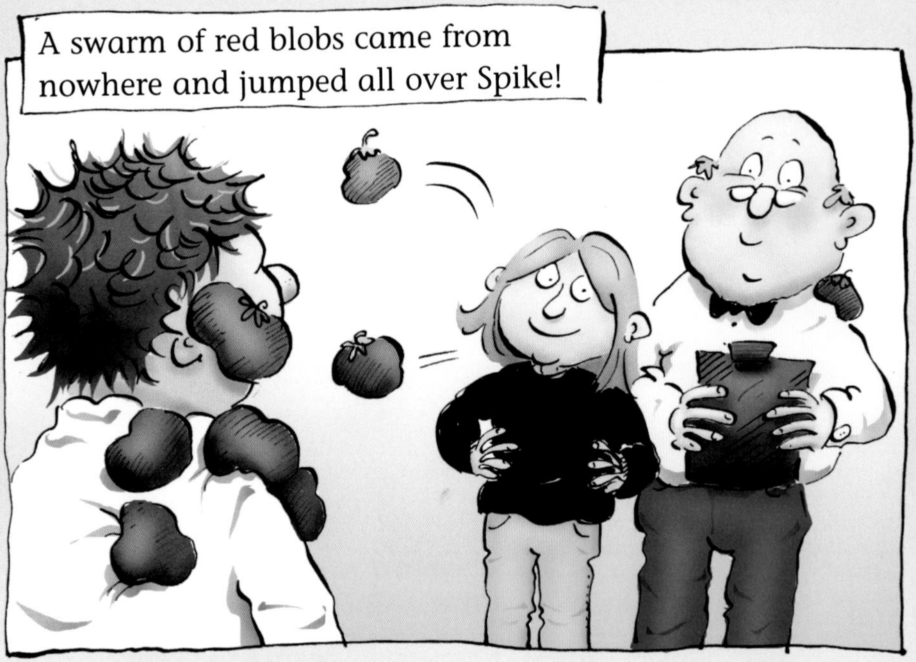

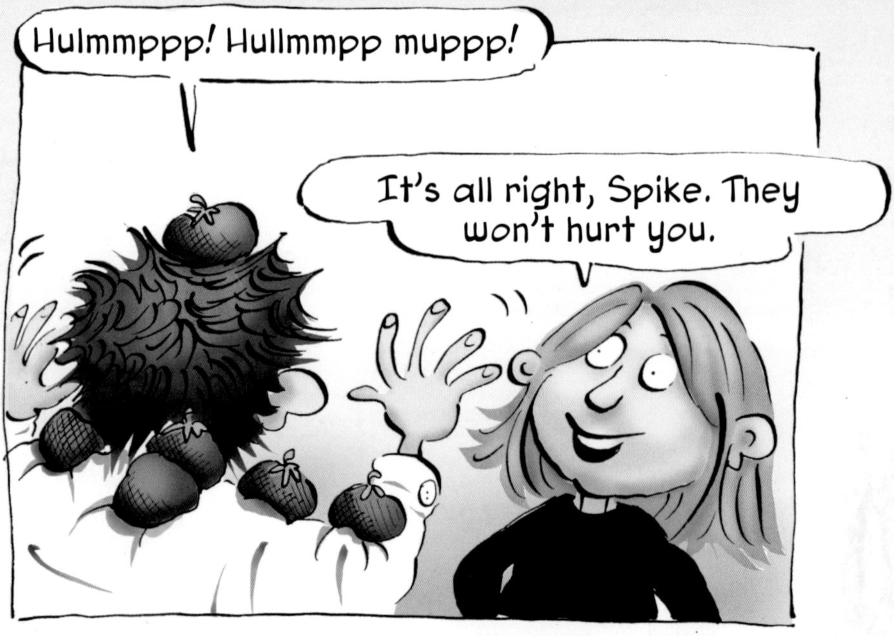
Hulmmppp! Hullmmpp muppp!
It's all right, Spike. They won't hurt you.

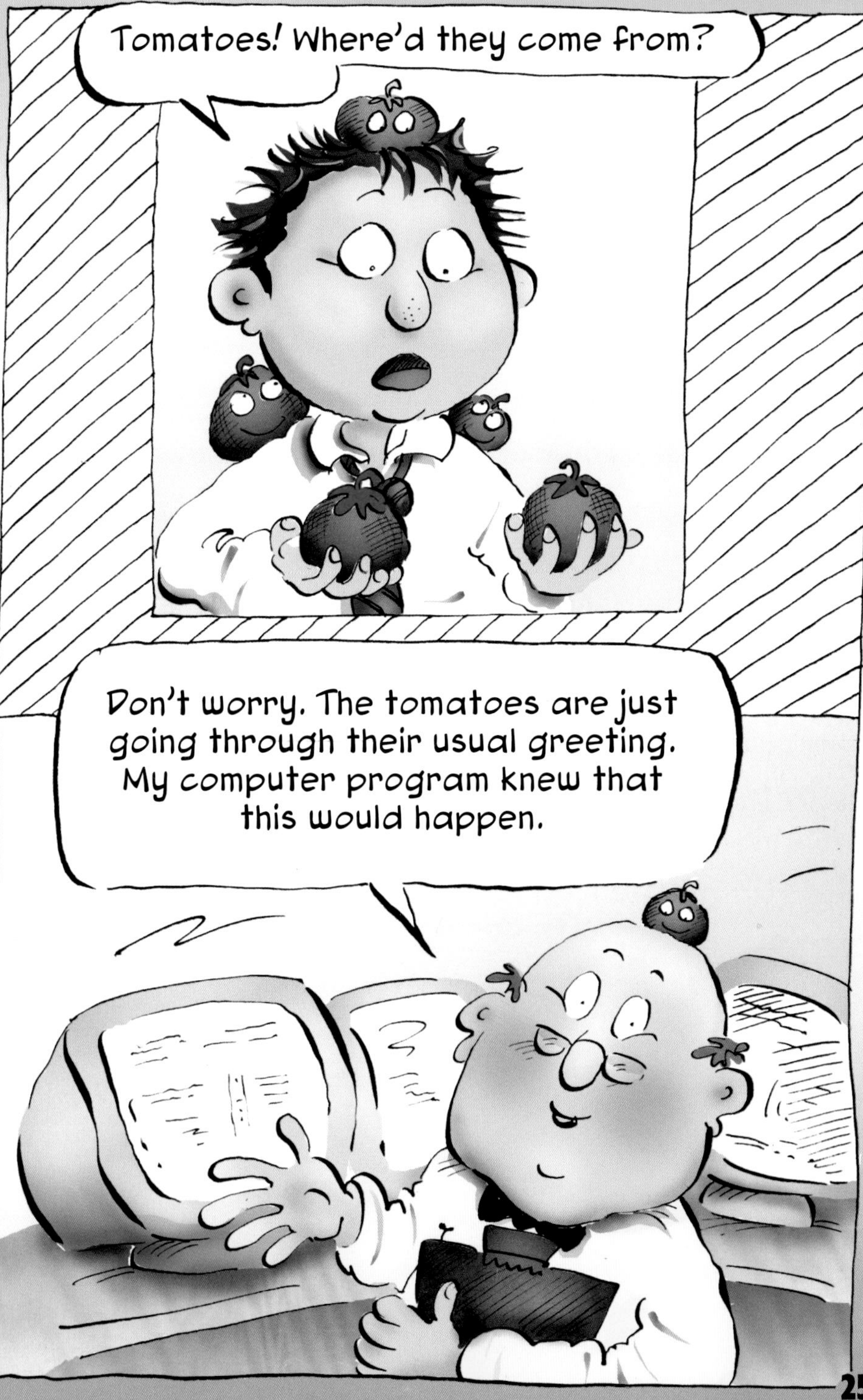
Tomatoes! Where'd they come from?
Don't worry. The tomatoes are just going through their usual greeting. My computer program knew that this would happen.

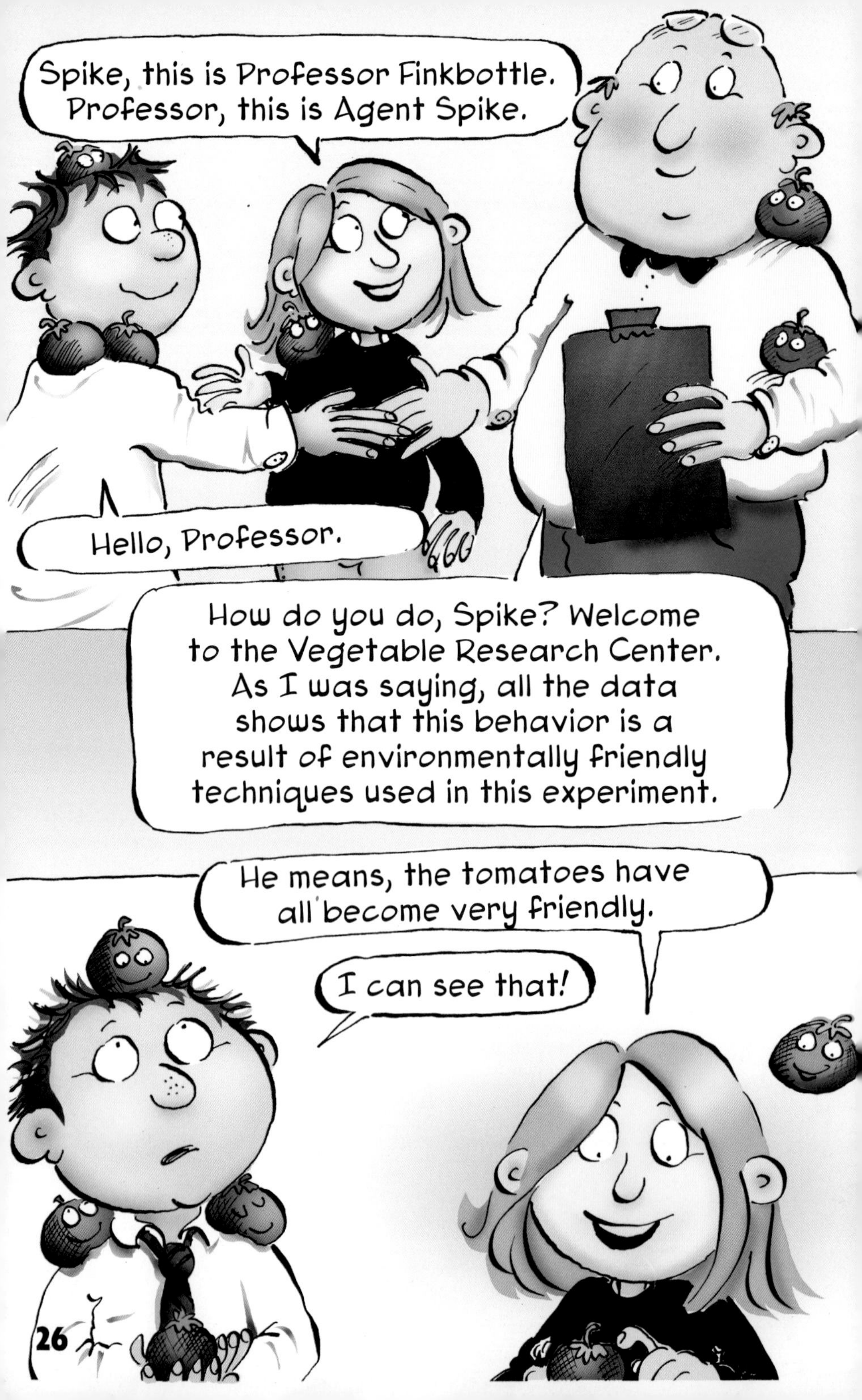
Spike, this is Professor Finkbottle. Professor, this is Agent Spike.
Hello, Professor.
How do you do, Spike? Welcome to the Vegetable Research Center. As I was saying, all the data shows that this behavior is a result of environmentally friendly techniques used in this experiment.
He means, the tomatoes have all become very friendly.
I can see that!

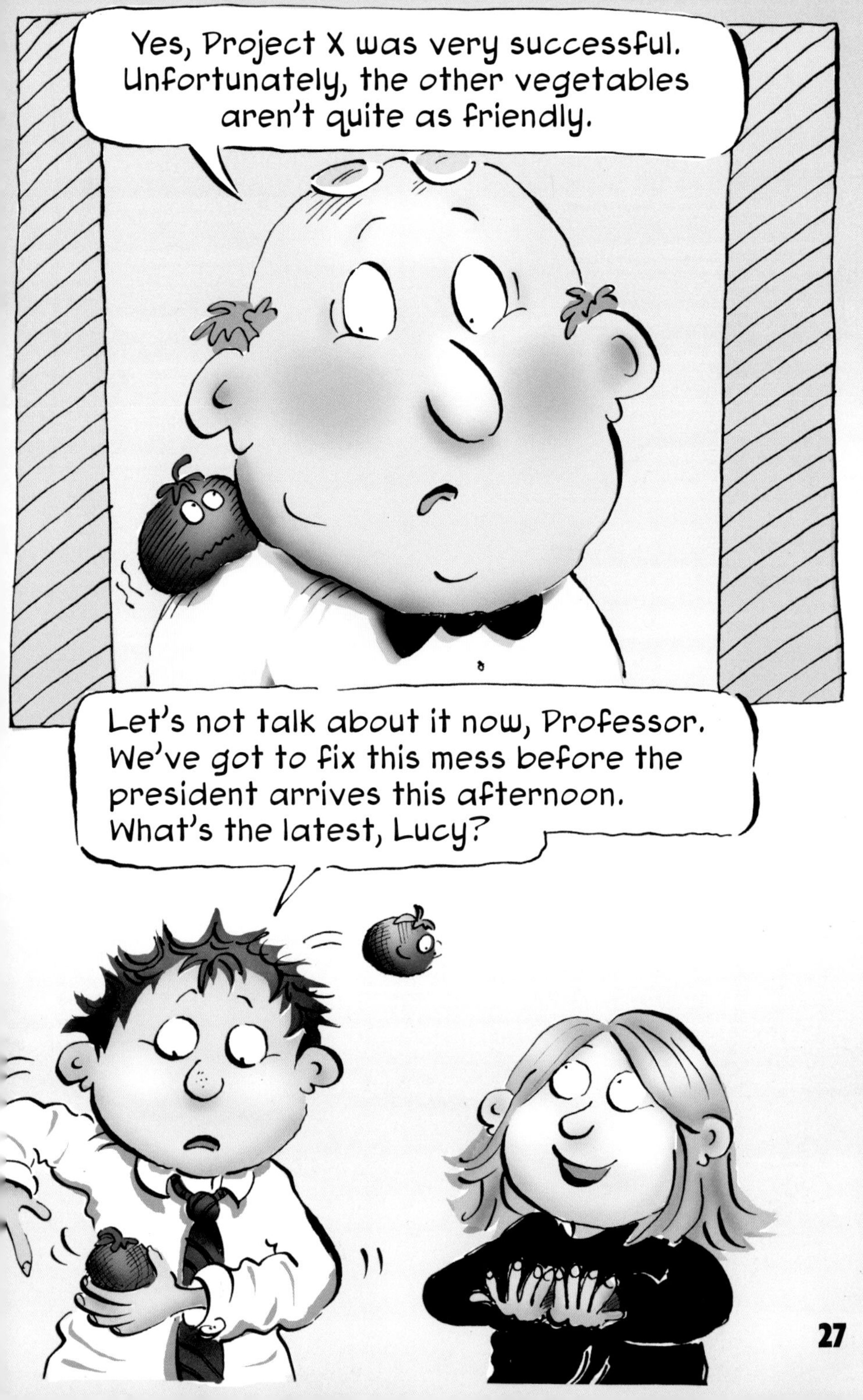
Yes, Project X was very successful. Unfortunately, the other vegetables aren't quite as friendly.
Let's not talk about it now, Professor. We've got to fix this mess before the president arrives this afternoon. What's the latest, Lucy?

The talking vegetables are being led by the Big Pumpkin. They are patrolling through the center and all the weeds are being sent to the compost bin.

I almost got sent there, too. Anything that isn't a vegetable is treated as a weed!

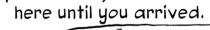

We hid in here and the Project X tomatoes saved us. They refused to join the Big Pumpkin. But guards were put outside, so we were stuck here until you arrived.

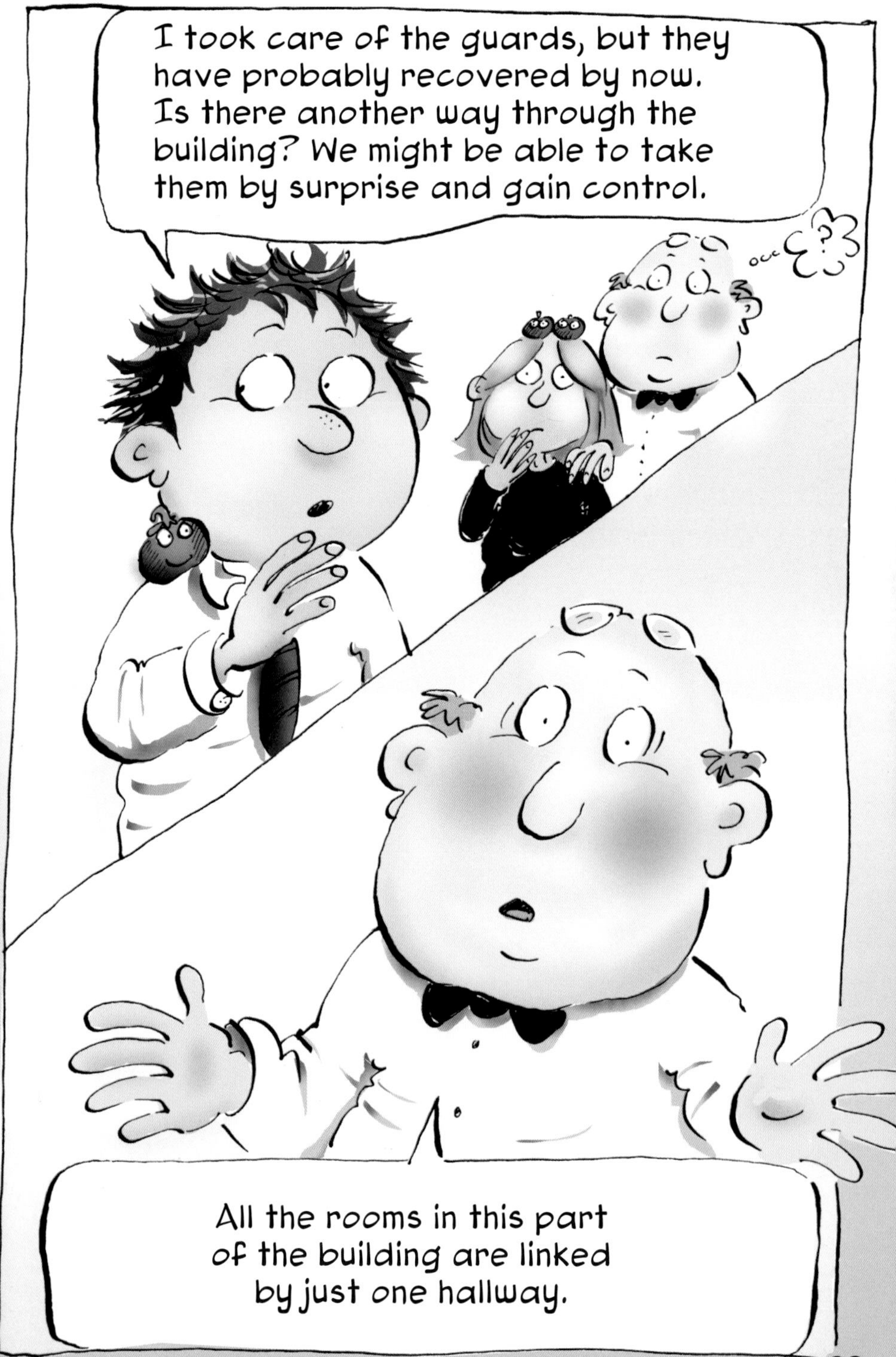
I took care of the guards, but they have probably recovered by now. Is there another way through the building? We might be able to take them by surprise and gain control.
?
All the rooms in this part of the building are linked by just one hallway.

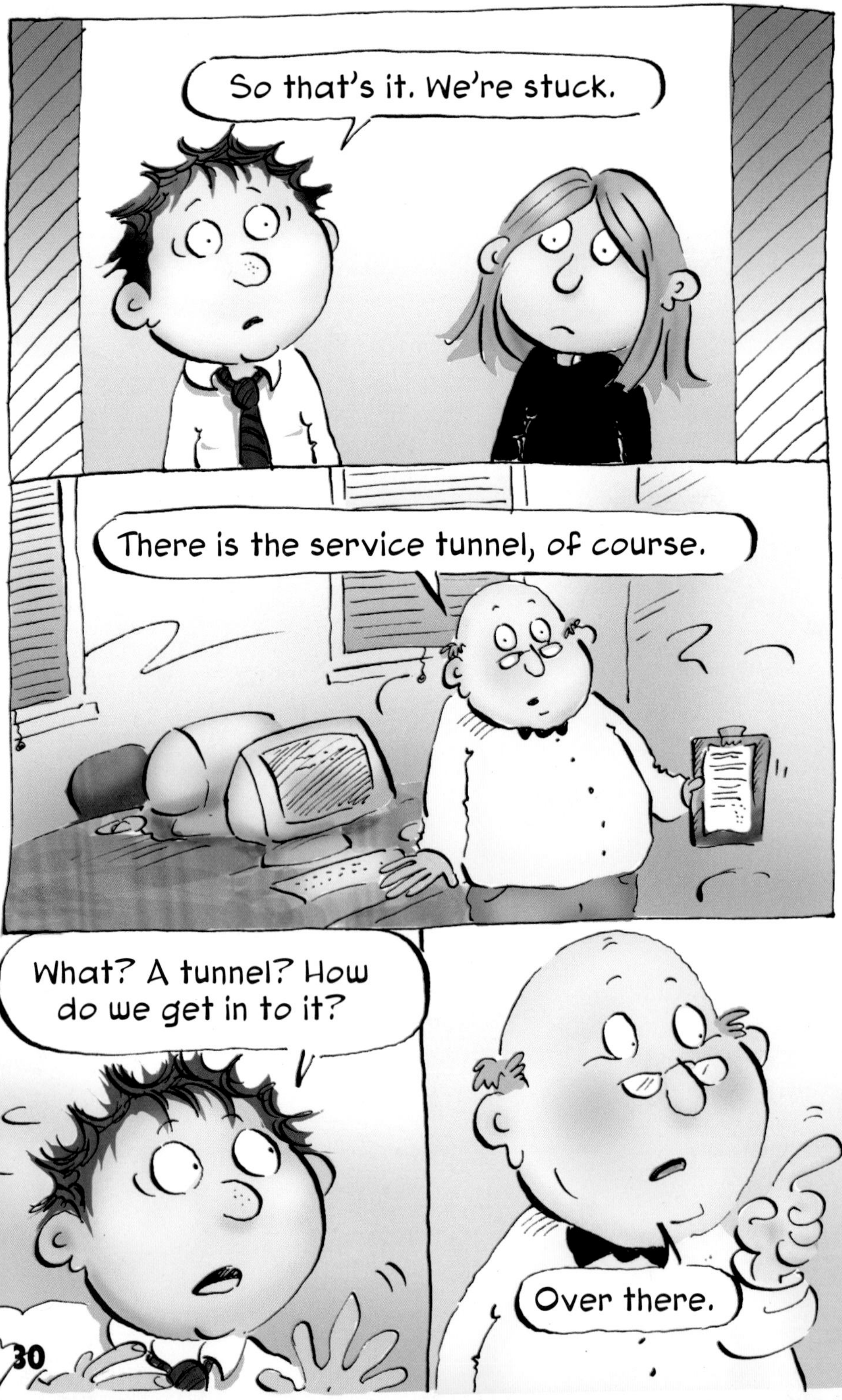
So that's it. We're stuck.
There is the service tunnel, of course.
What? A tunnel? How do we get in to it?
Over there.

Chapter Five

They ran to the spot where Professor Finkbottle was pointing. Spike lifted the hatch.

What about the tomatoes?

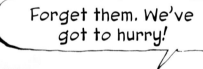

Forget them. We've got to hurry!

Let me talk to them.

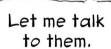

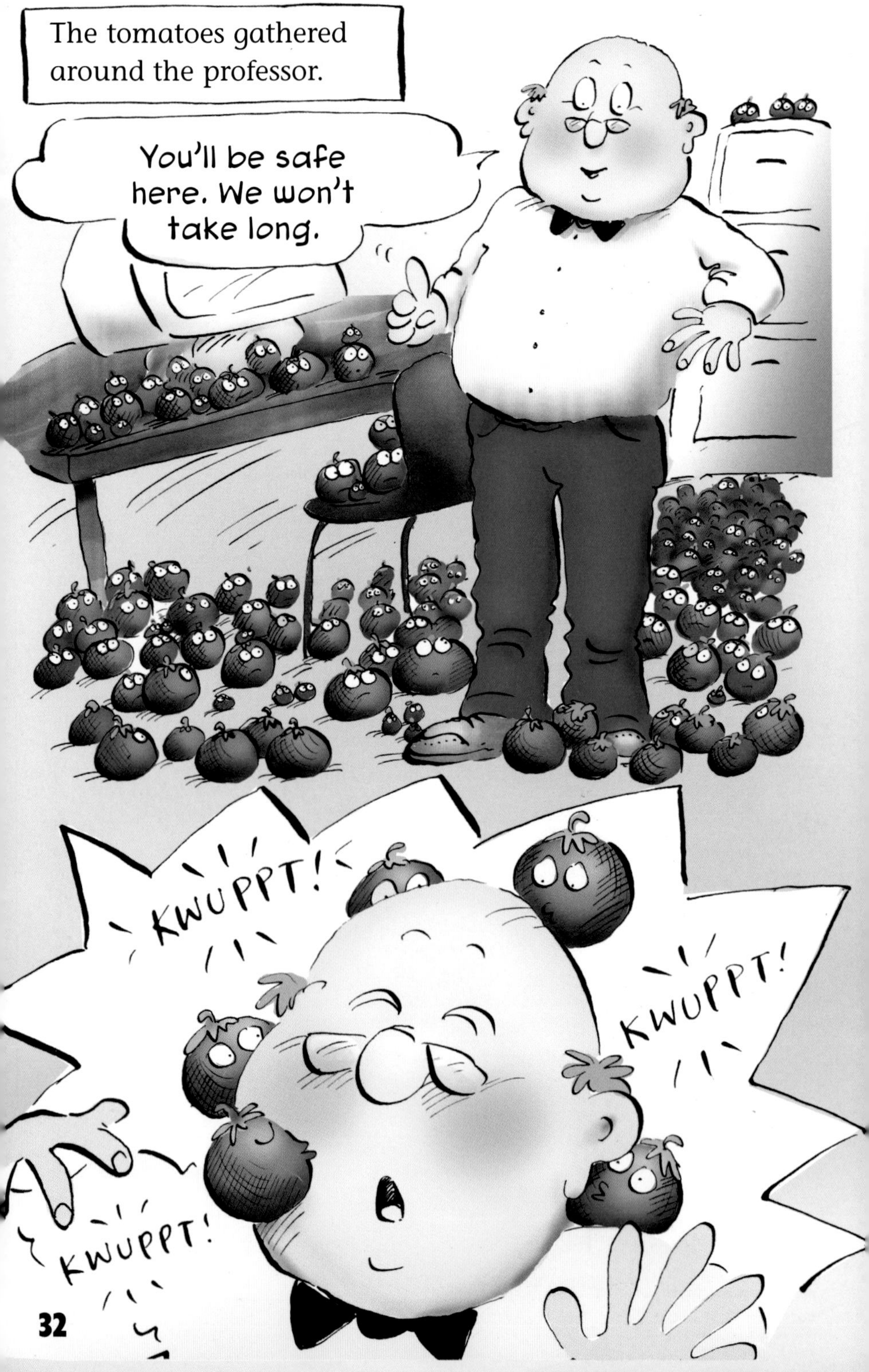
The tomatoes gathered around the professor.
You'll be safe here. We won't take long.
KWUPPT!
KWUPPT!
KWUPPT!

Spike climbed down a ladder, into the tunnel. Then the professor and Lucy followed him.

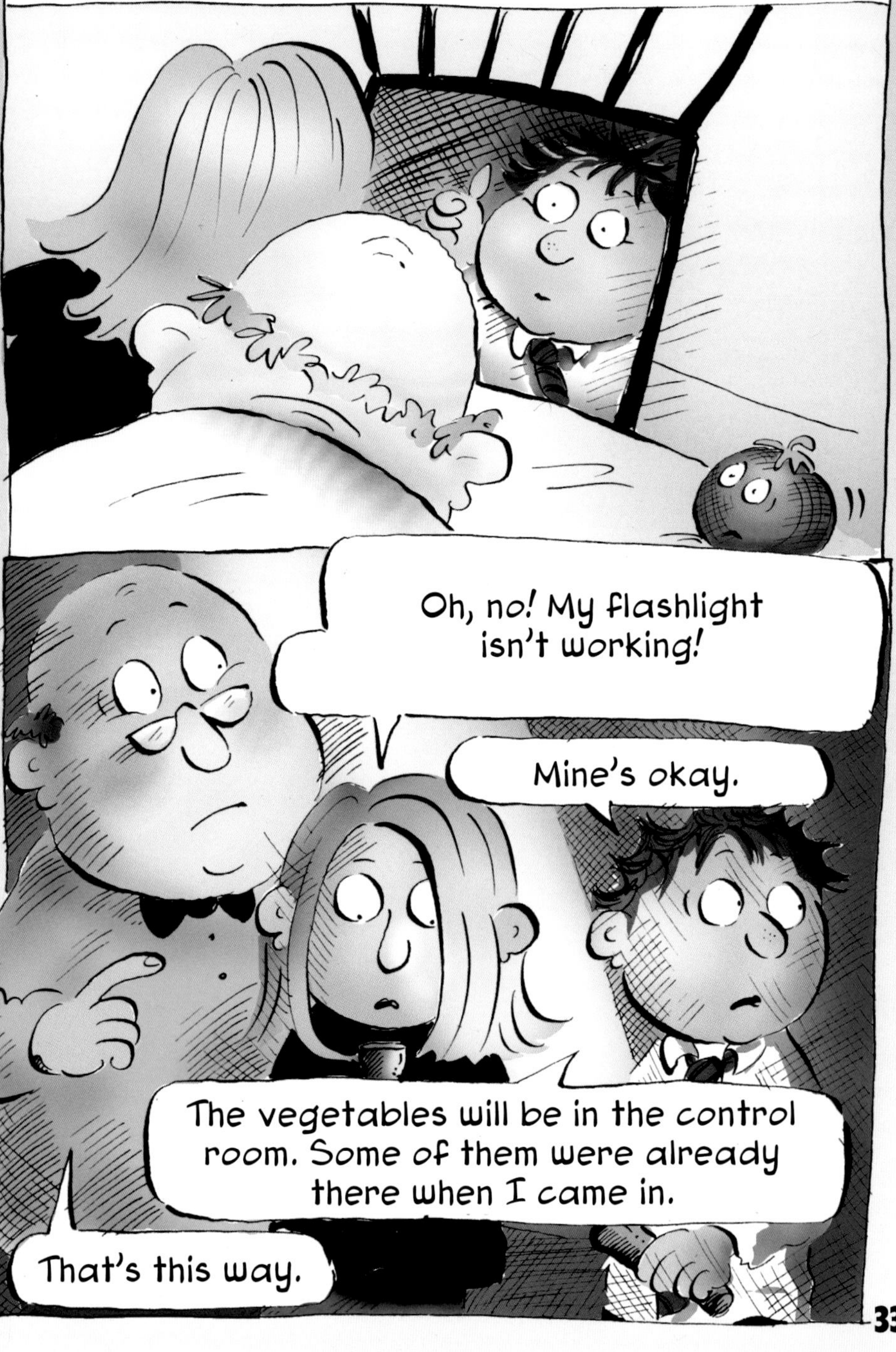
Oh, no! My flashlight isn't working!
Mine's okay.
The vegetables will be in the control room. Some of them were already there when I came in.
That's this way.

Spike turned on his flashlight, and the group crawled through the tunnel. It was cramped with cables and pipes everywhere.

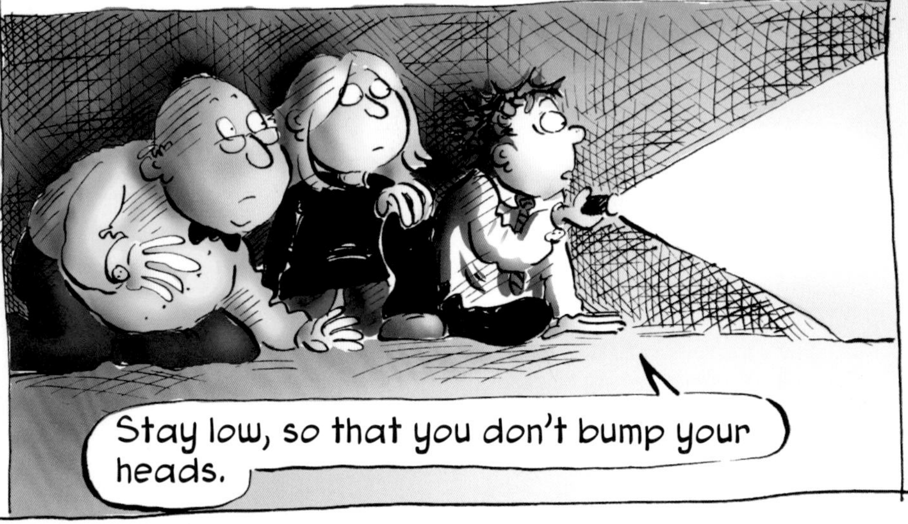
Stay low, so that you don't bump your heads.

The professor bumped his head.

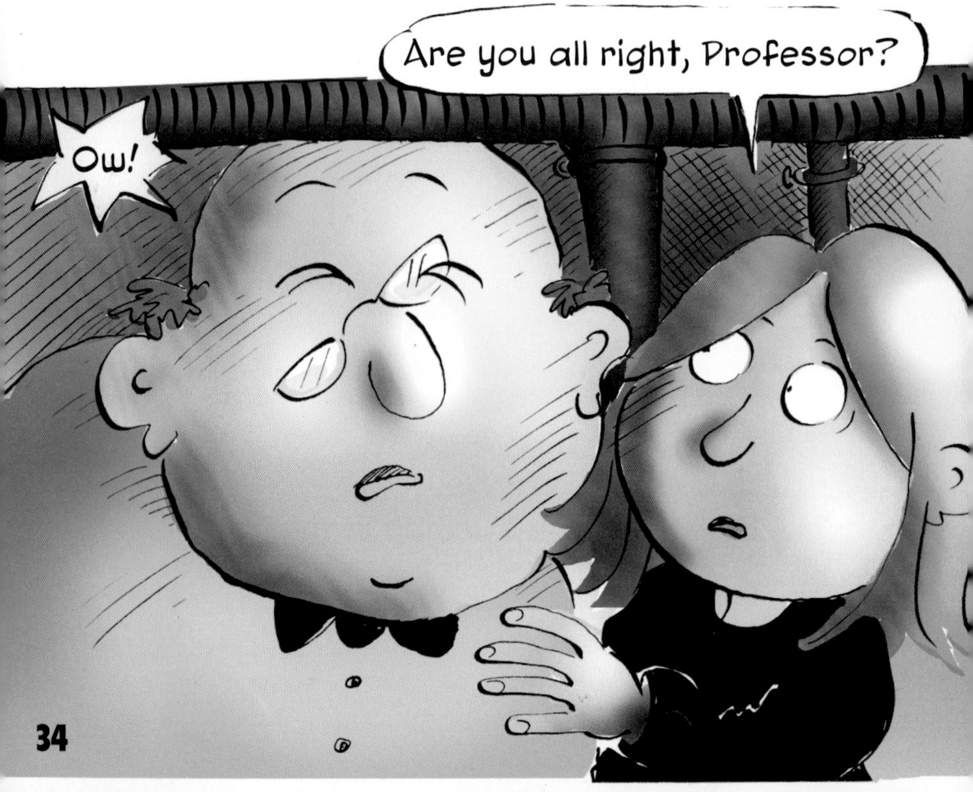
Are you all right, Professor?
Ow!

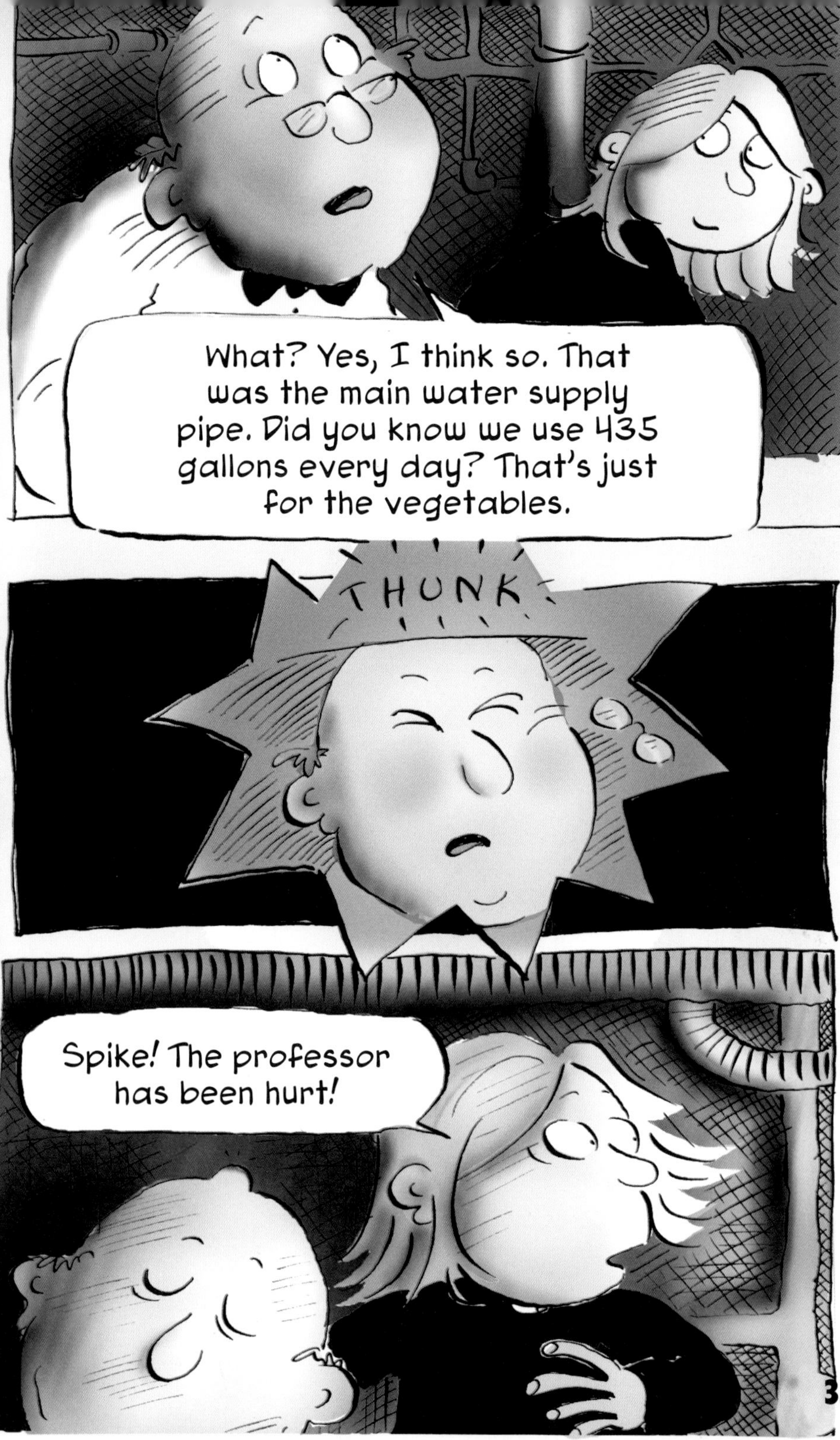
What? Yes, I think so. That was the main water supply pipe. Did you know we use 435 gallons every day? That's just for the vegetables.
THUNK
Spike! The professor has been hurt!

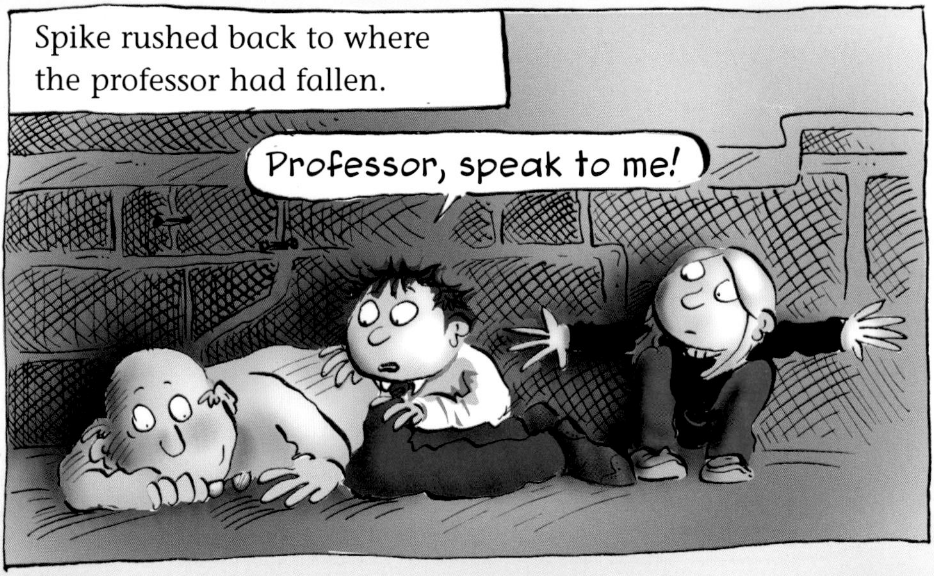
Spike rushed back to where the professor had fallen.
Professor, speak to me!

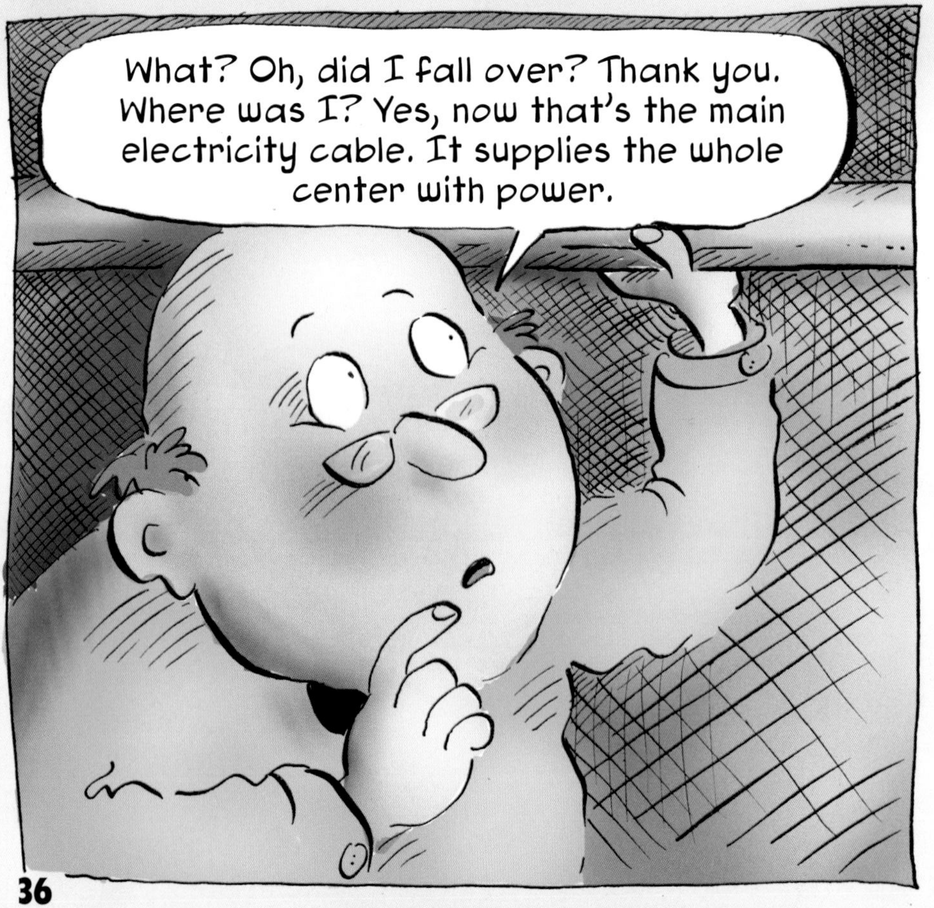
What? Oh, did I fall over? Thank you. Where was I? Yes, now that's the main electricity cable. It supplies the whole center with power.

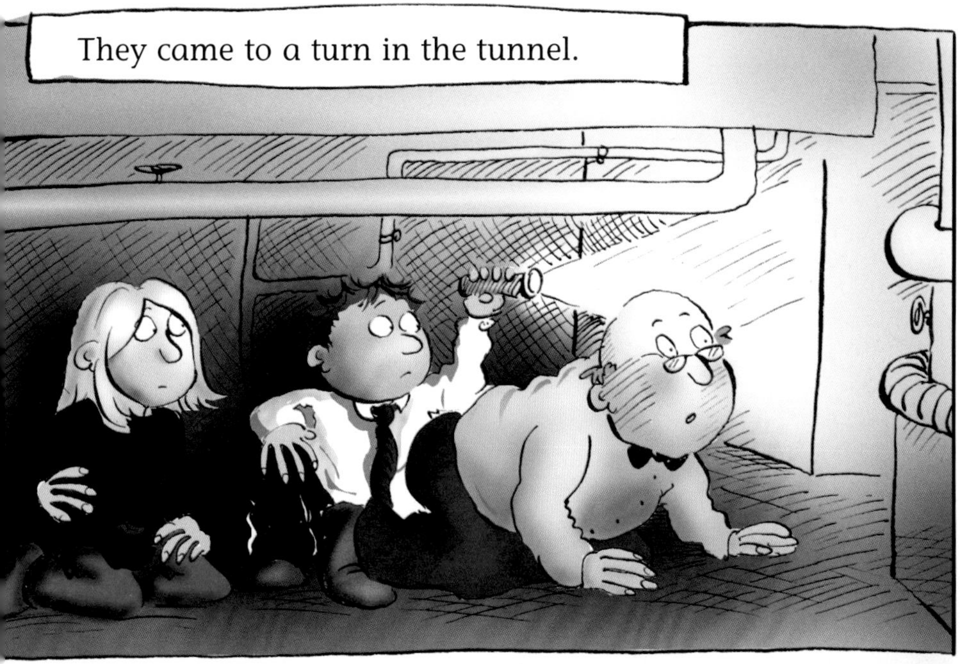
They came to a turn in the tunnel.

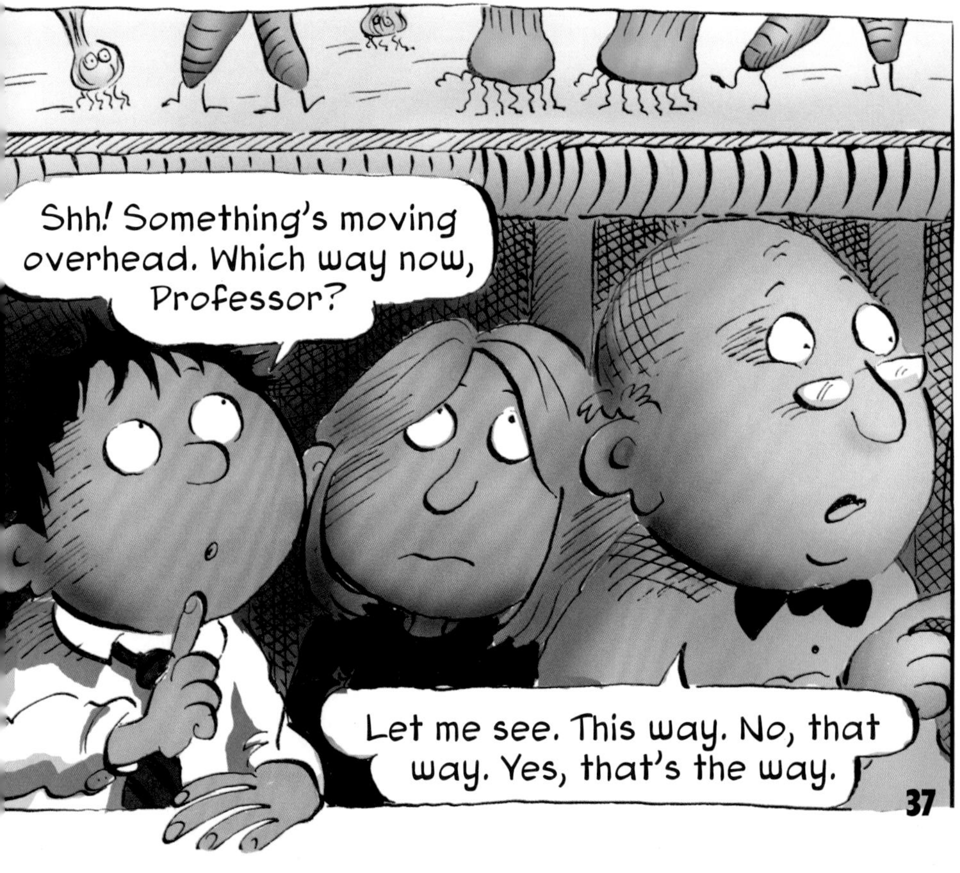
Shh! Something's moving overhead. Which way now, Professor?
Let me see. This way. No, that way. Yes, that's the way.

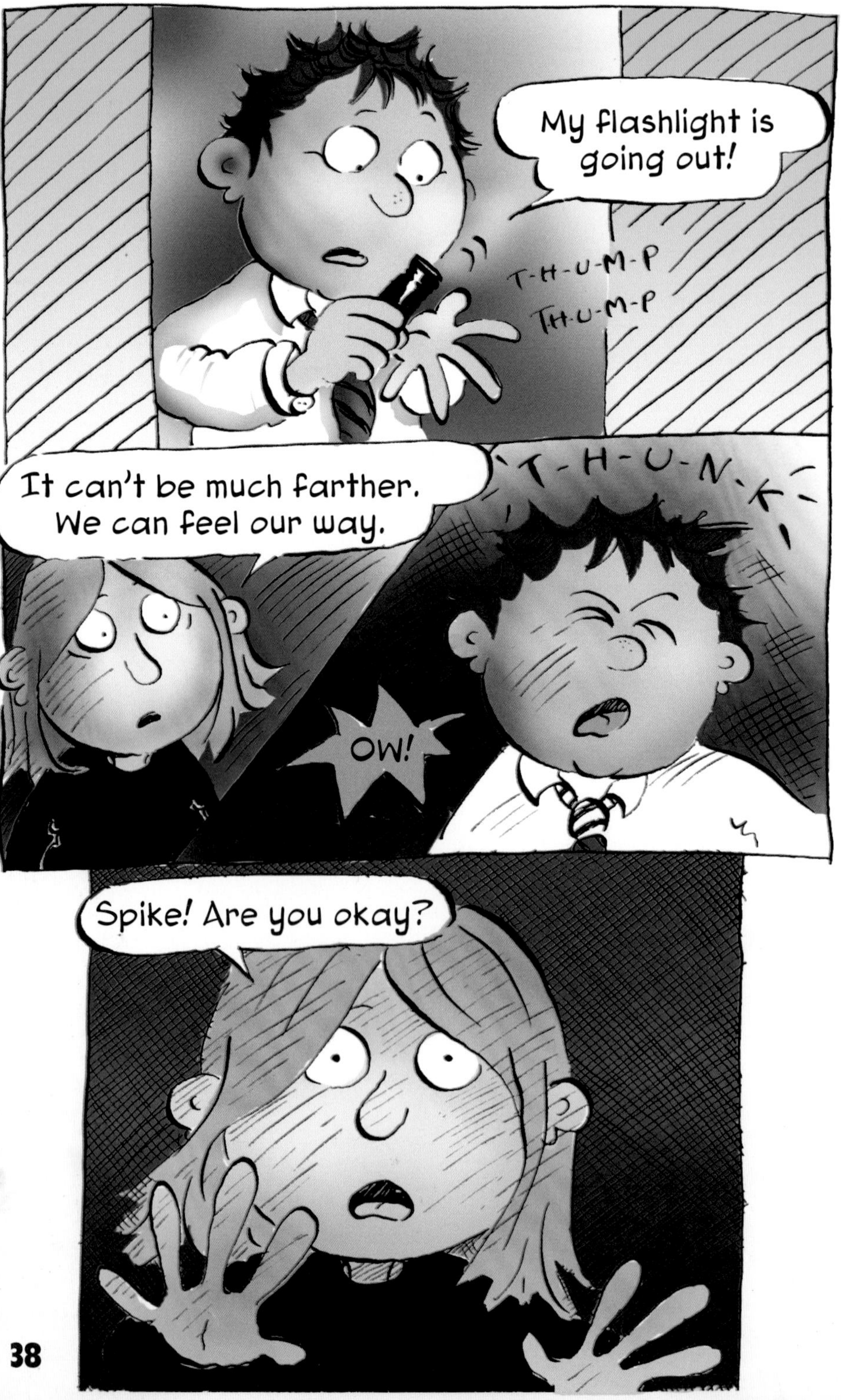
My flashlight is going out!
T-H-U-M-P
TH-U-M-P
It can't be much farther. We can feel our way.
T-H-U-N-K
OW!
Spike! Are you okay?

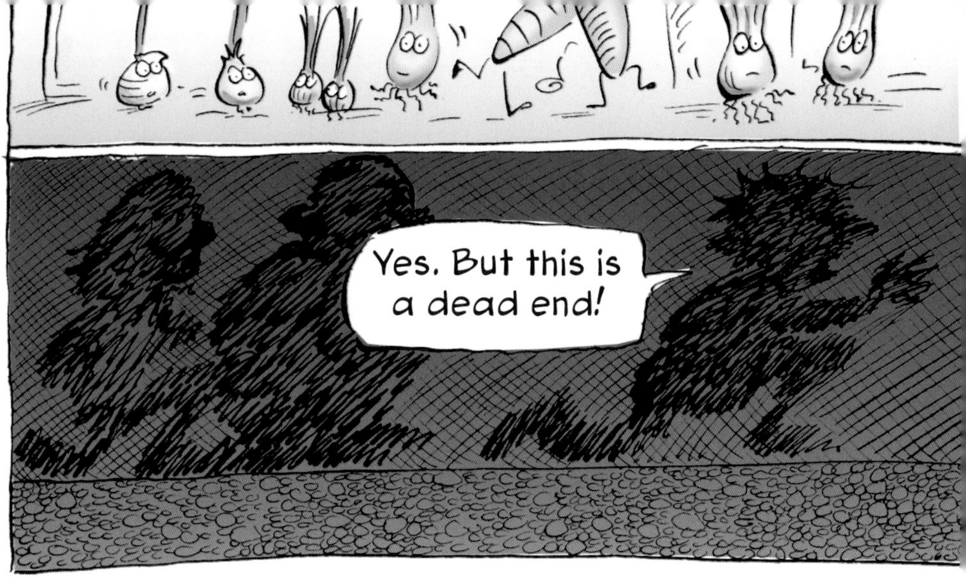
Yes. But this is
a dead end!

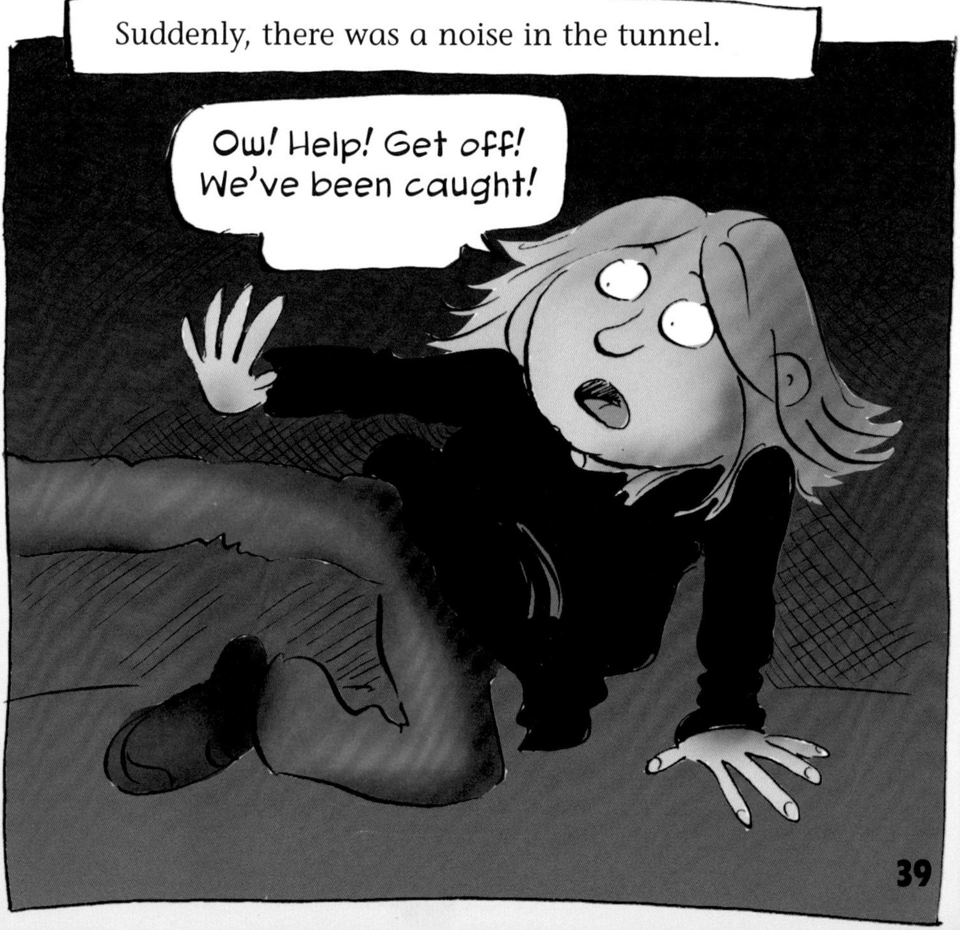
Suddenly, there was a noise in the tunnel.
Ow! Help! Get off!
We've been caught!

Chapter Six

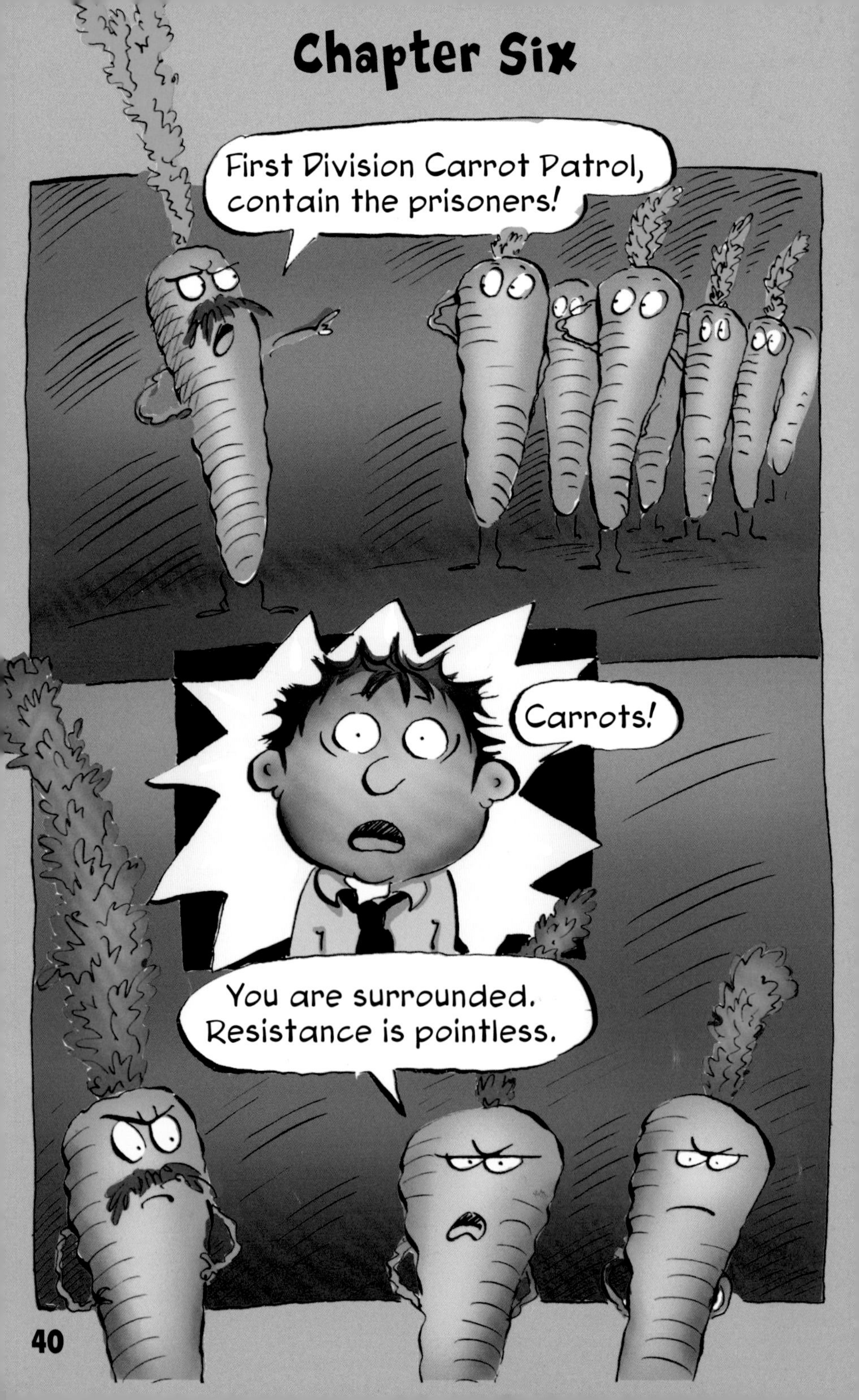
First Division Carrot Patrol, contain the prisoners!
Carrots!
You are surrounded. Resistance is pointless.

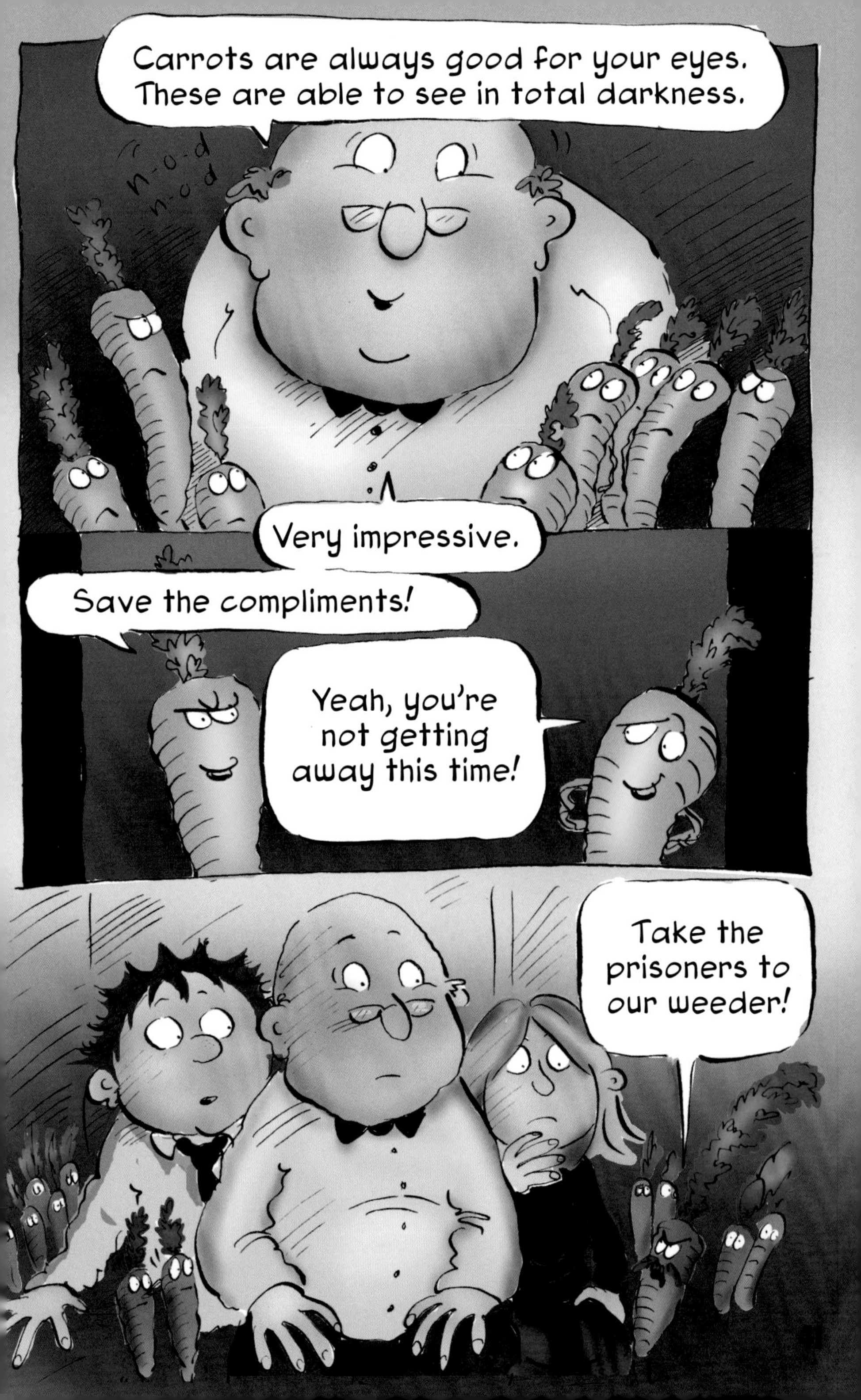
Carrots are always good for your eyes. These are able to see in total darkness.
n-o-d n-o-d
Very impressive.
Save the compliments!
Yeah, you're not getting away this time!
Take the prisoners to our weeder!

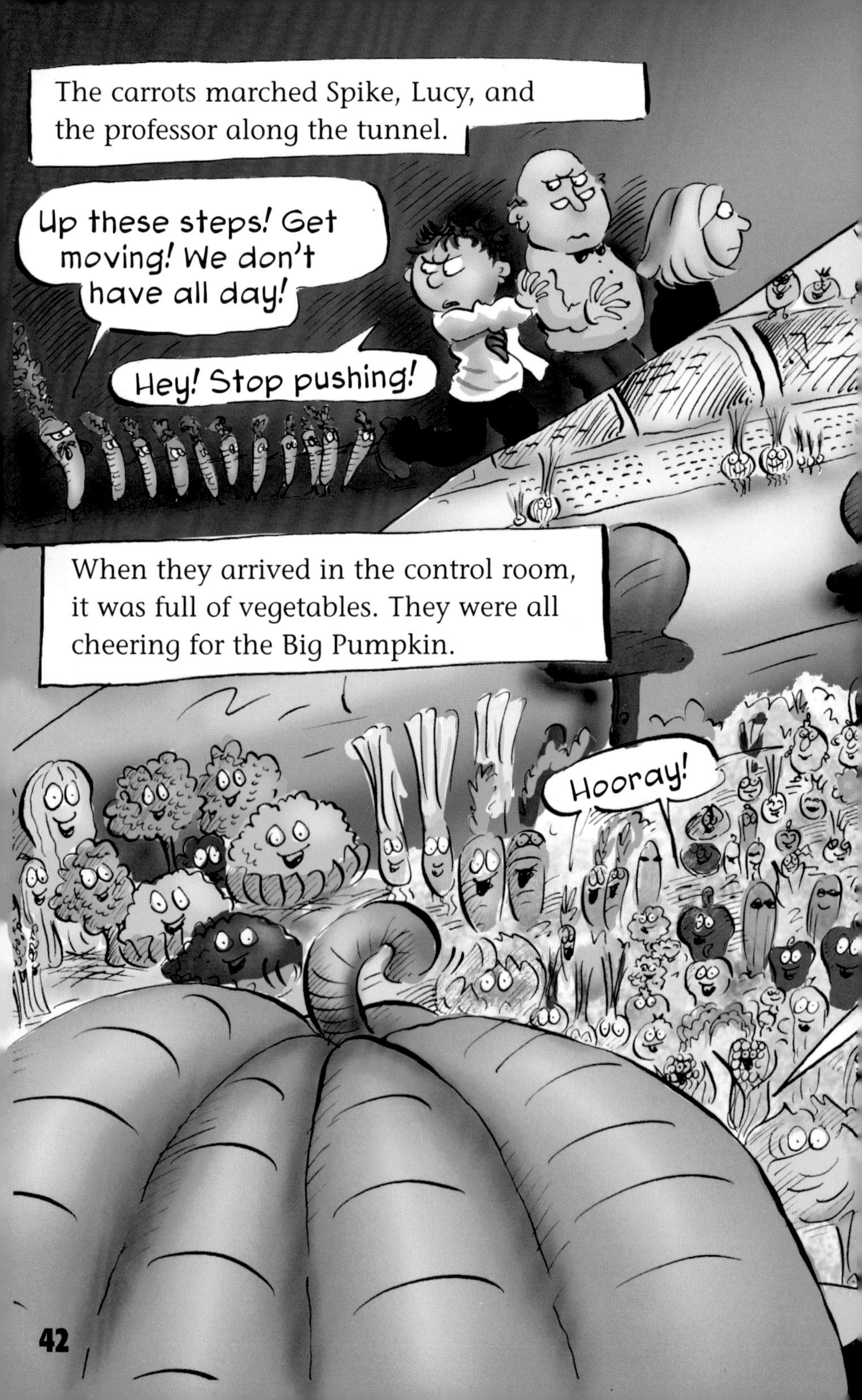
The carrots marched Spike, Lucy, and the professor along the tunnel.
Up these steps! Get moving! We don't have all day!
Hey! Stop pushing!
When they arrived in the control room, it was full of vegetables. They were all cheering for the Big Pumpkin.
Hooray!

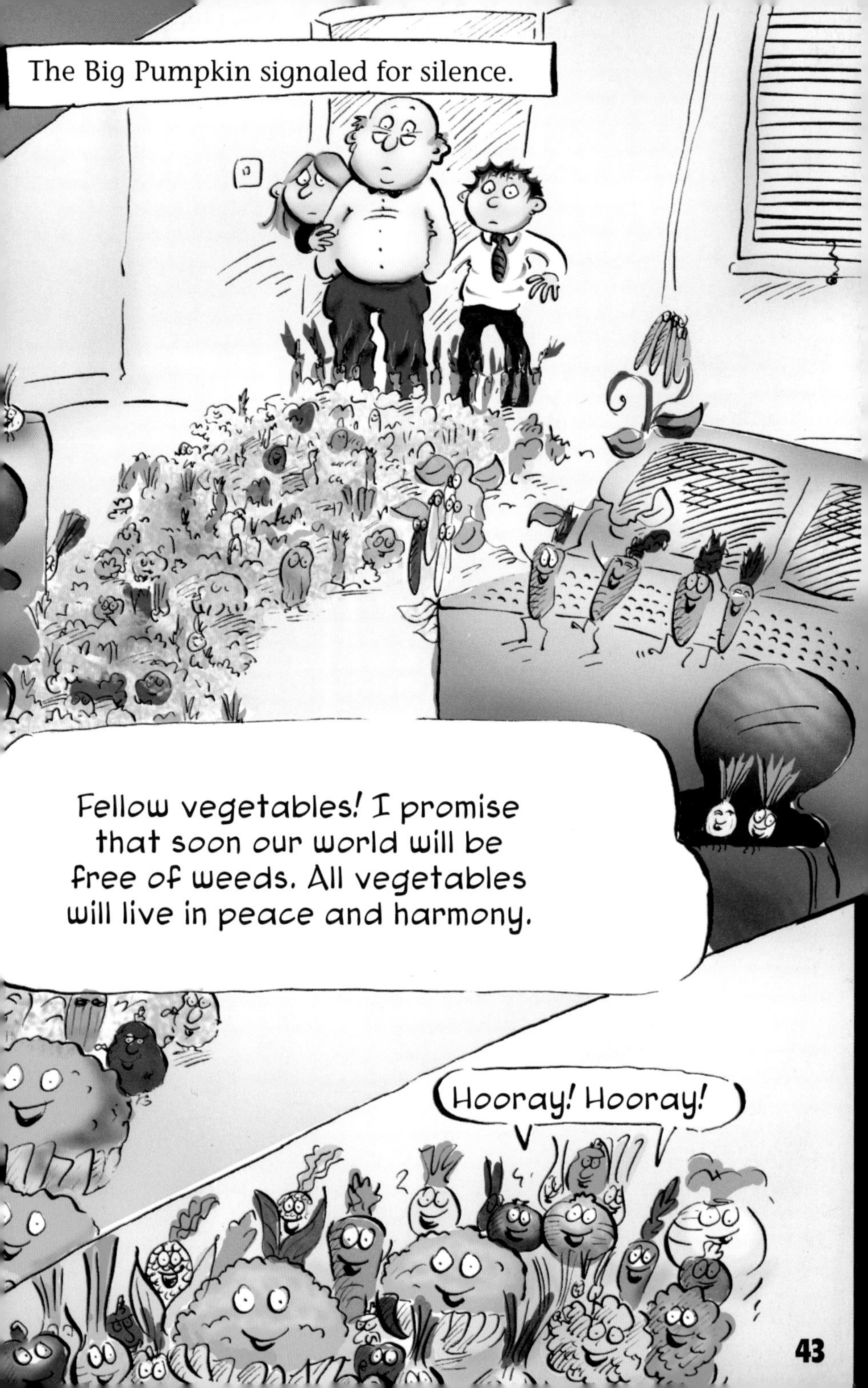
The Big Pumpkin signaled for silence.
Fellow vegetables! I promise that soon our world will be free of weeds. All vegetables will live in peace and harmony.
Hooray! Hooray!

The carrots pushed their prisoners to the front.

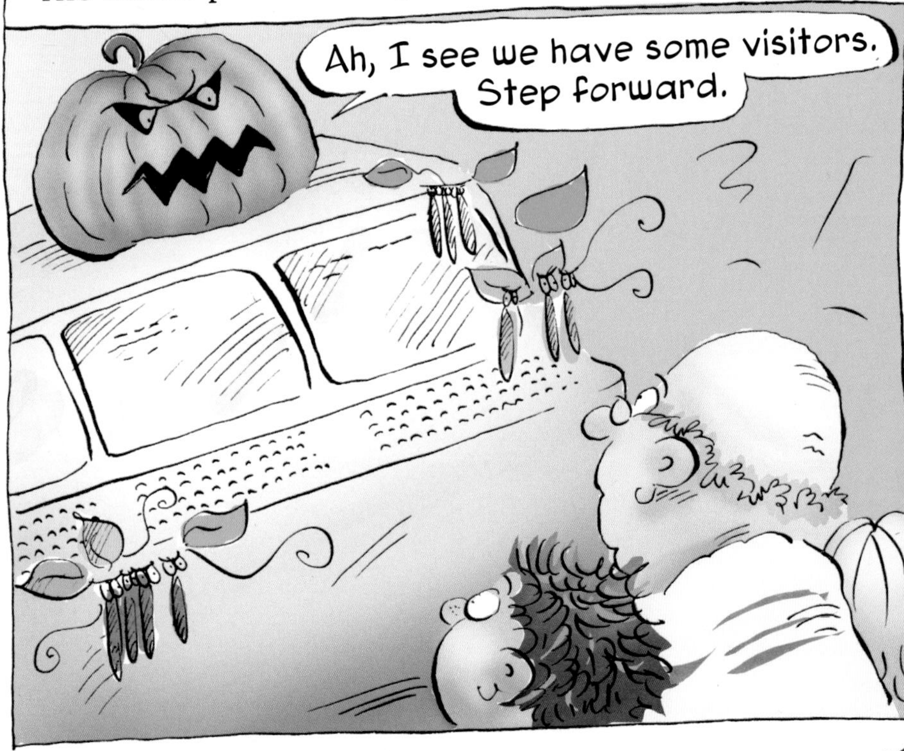
Ah, I see we have some visitors. Step forward.

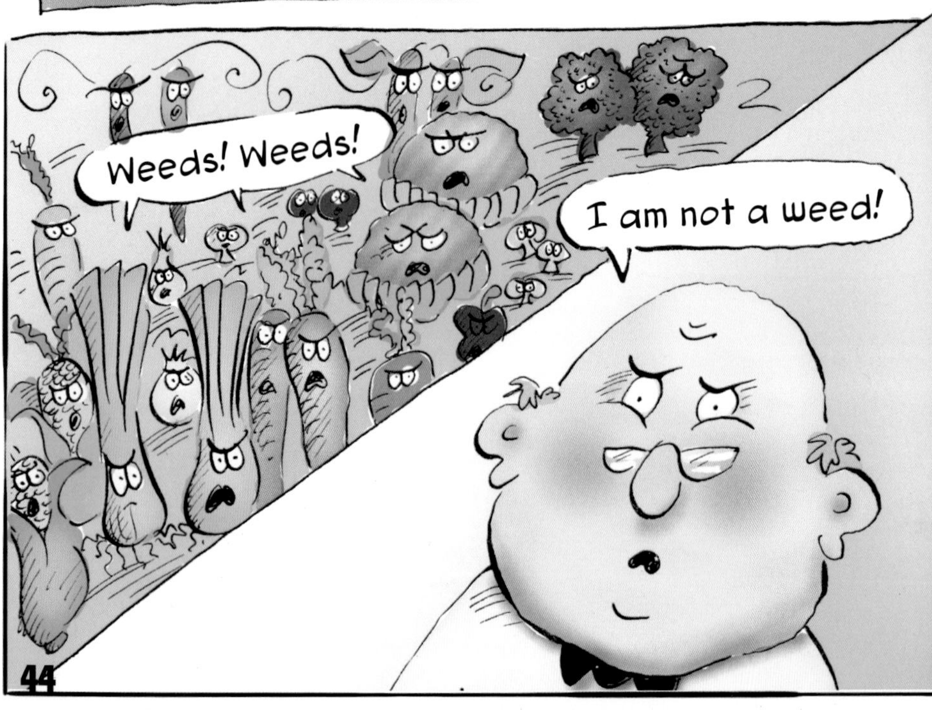
Weeds! Weeds!
I am not a weed!

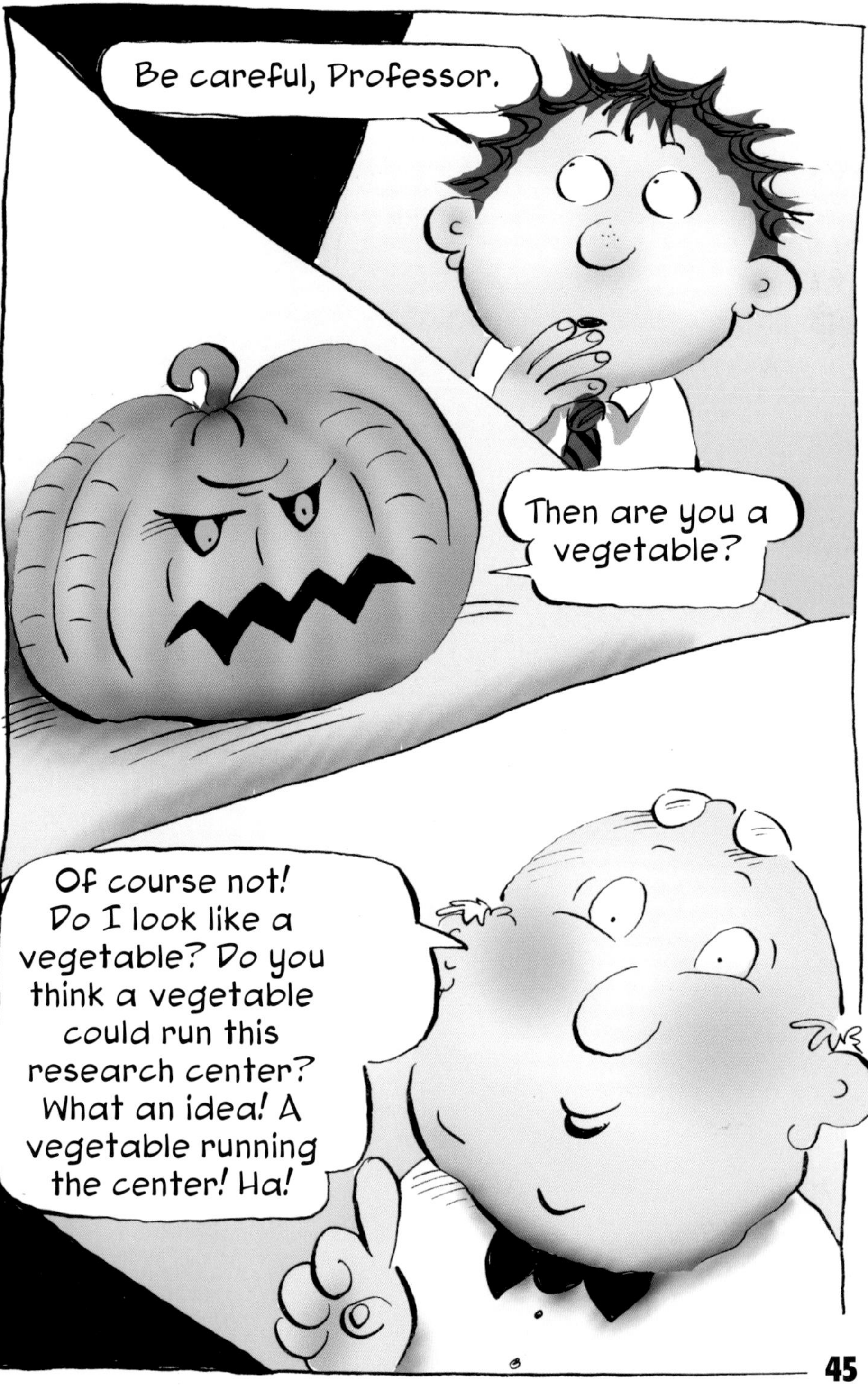
Be careful, Professor.
Then are you a vegetable?
Of course not! Do I look like a vegetable? Do you think a vegetable could run this research center? What an idea! A vegetable running the center! Ha!

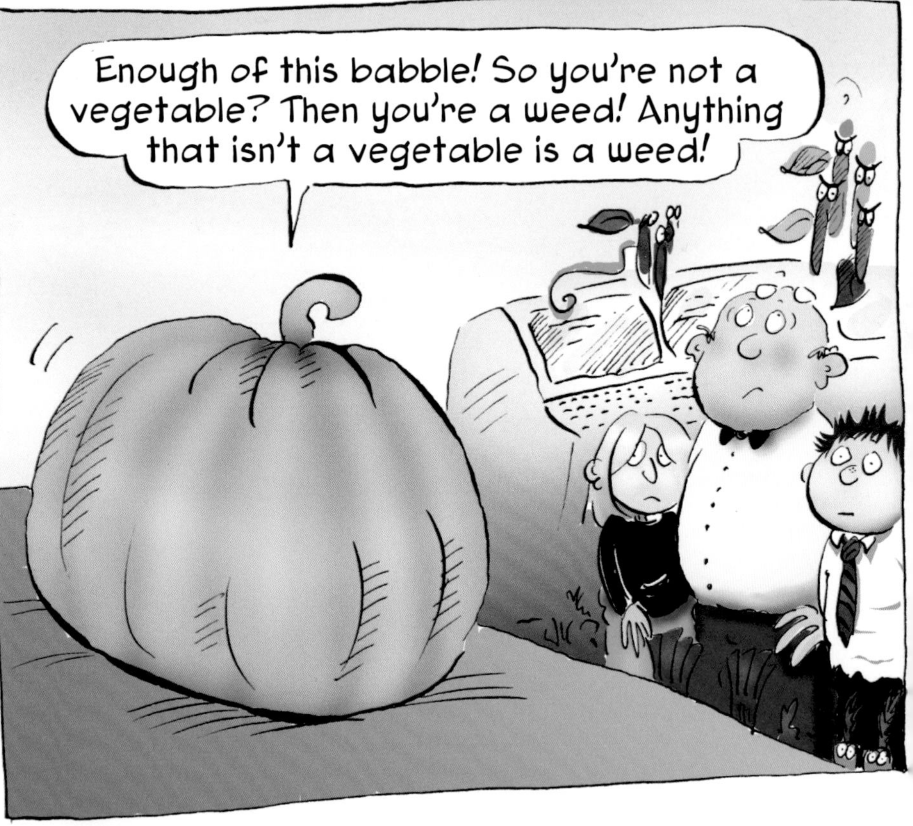
Enough of this babble! So you're not a vegetable? Then you're a weed! Anything that isn't a vegetable is a weed!

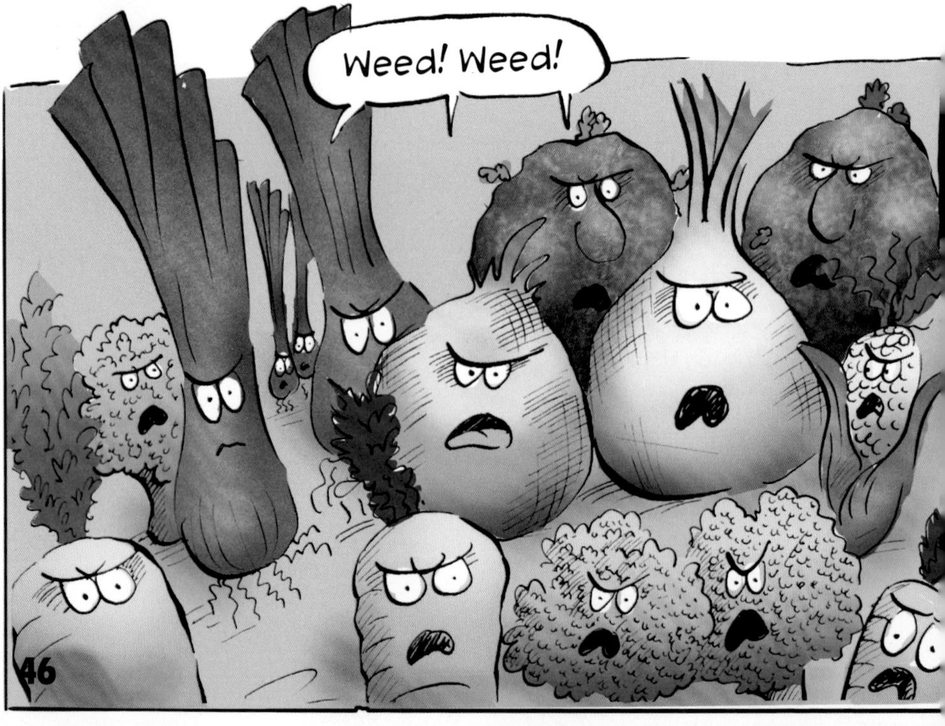
Weed! Weed!

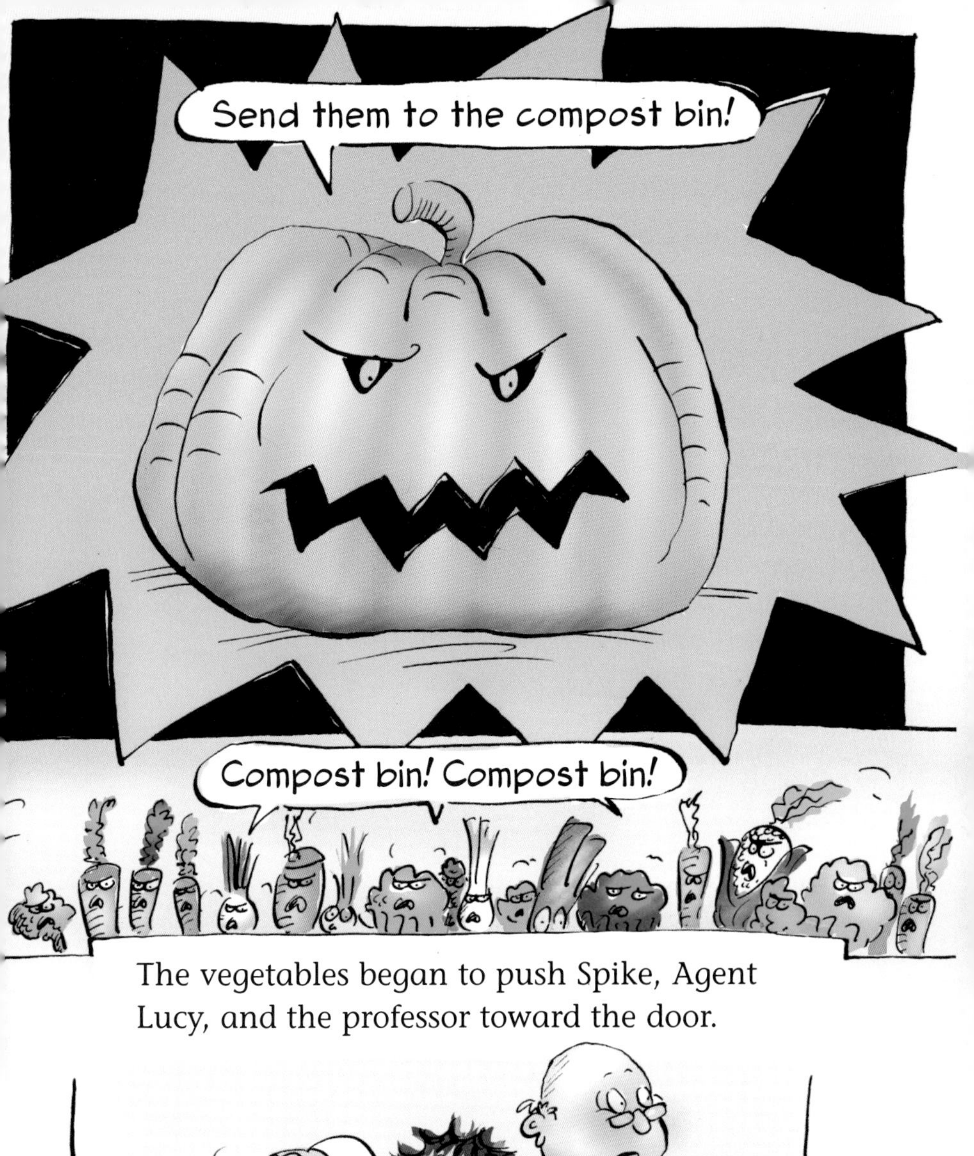
Send them to the compost bin!
Compost bin! Compost bin!

The vegetables began to push Spike, Agent Lucy, and the professor toward the door.

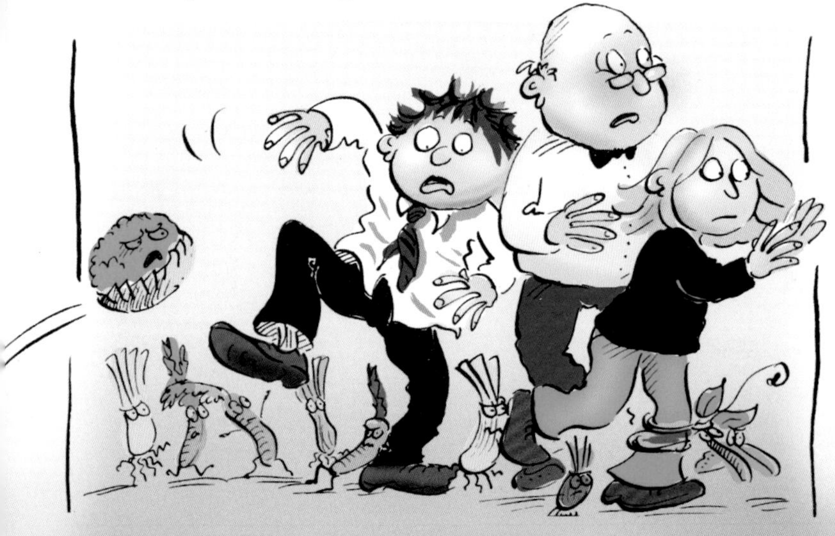

Chapter Seven

Spike was thinking fast. How could he get them out of this mess? Then suddenly, he had an idea.

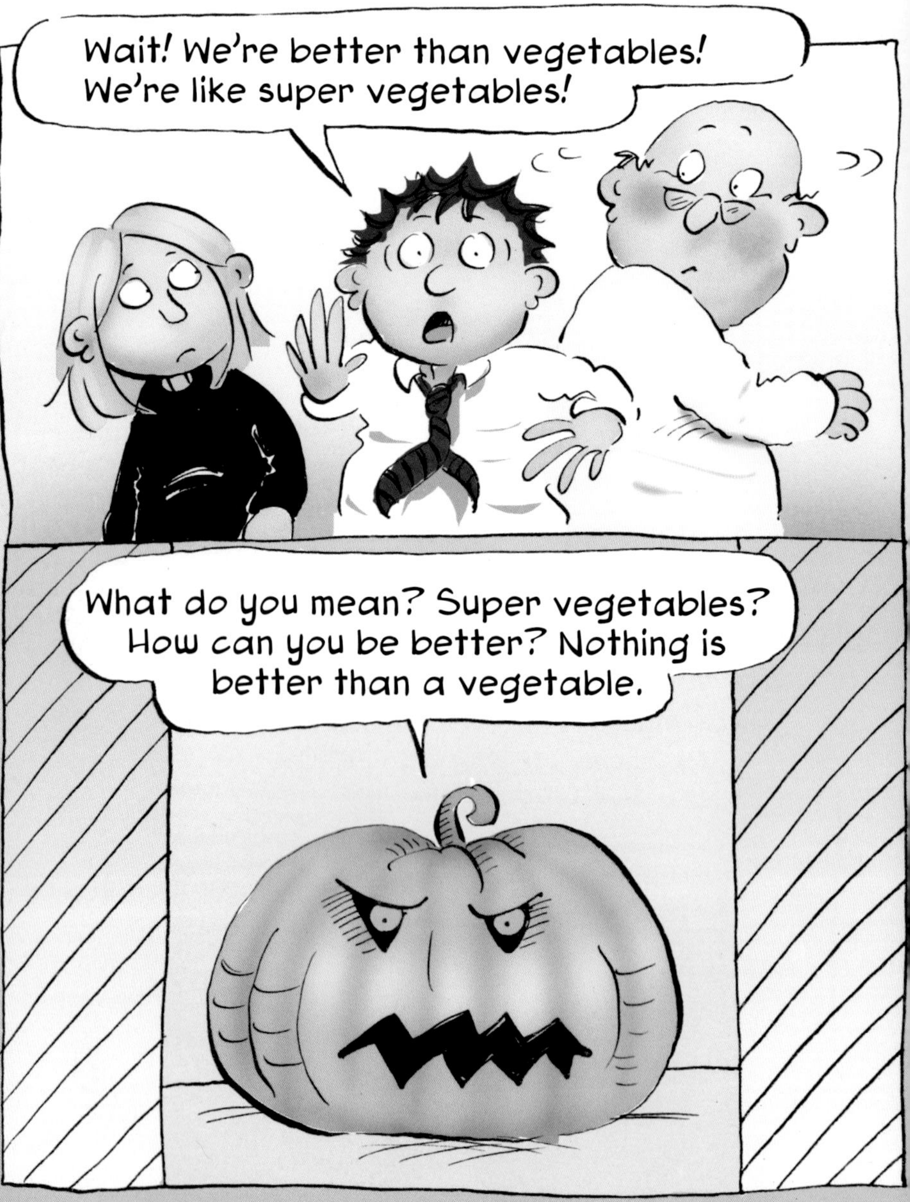
Wait! We're better than vegetables! We're like super vegetables!
What do you mean? Super vegetables? How can you be better? Nothing is better than a vegetable.

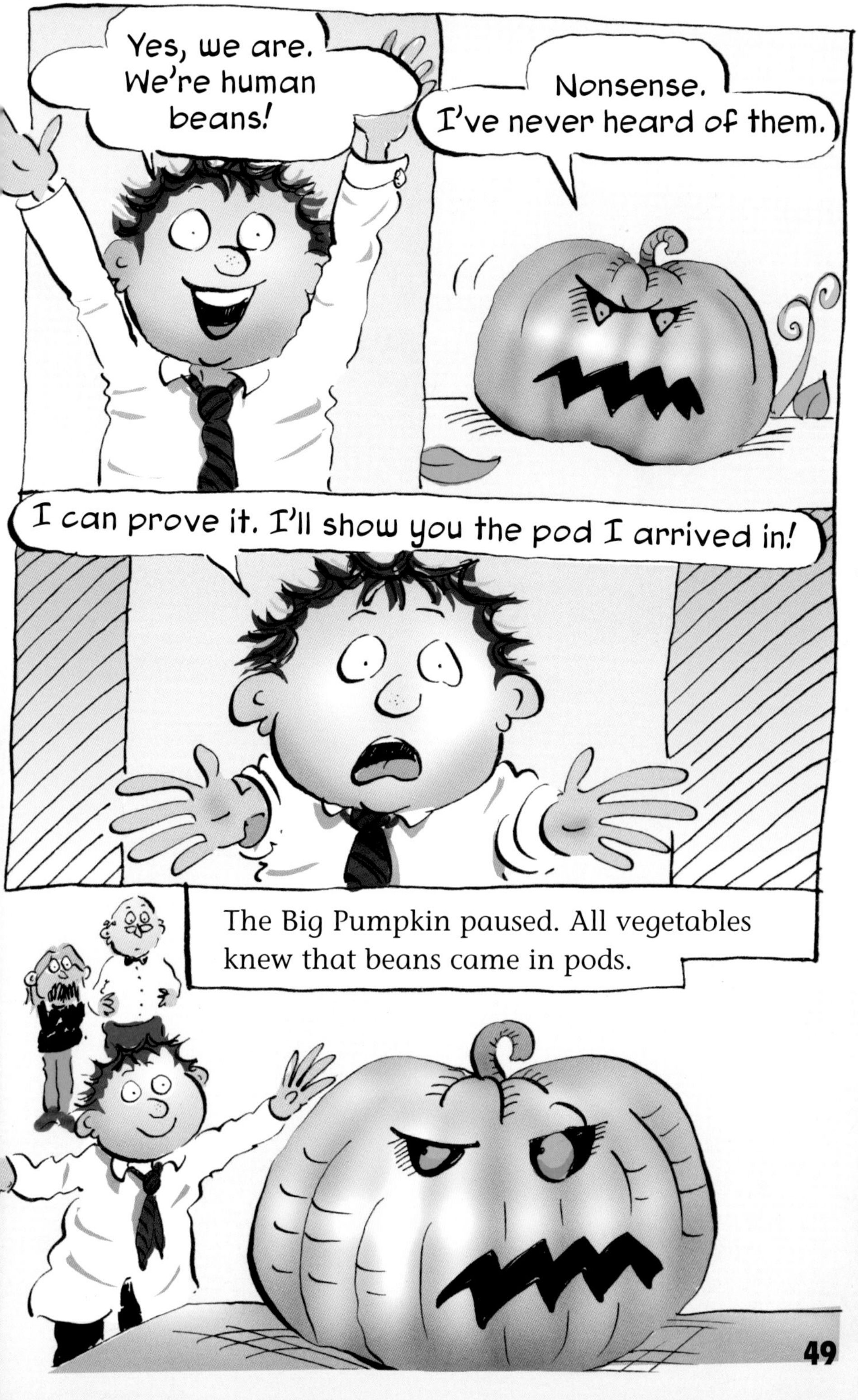
Yes, we are. We're human beans!
Nonsense. I've never heard of them.
I can prove it. I'll show you the pod I arrived in!
The Big Pumpkin paused. All vegetables knew that beans came in pods.

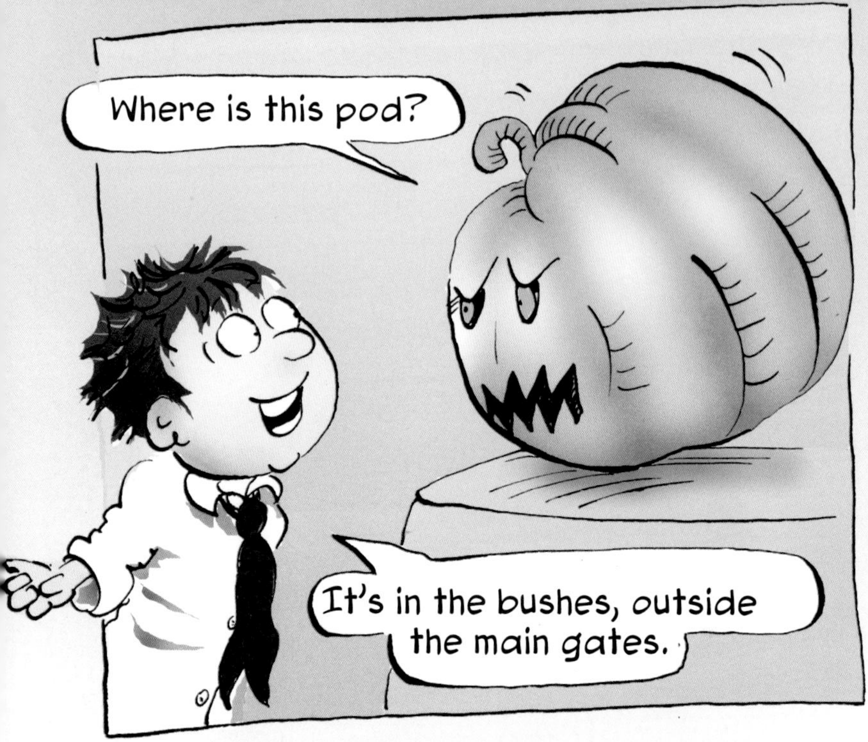
Where is this pod?
It's in the bushes, outside the main gates.

The Big Pumpkin sent a couple of cucumbers to find the pod. Everybody went outside to wait.

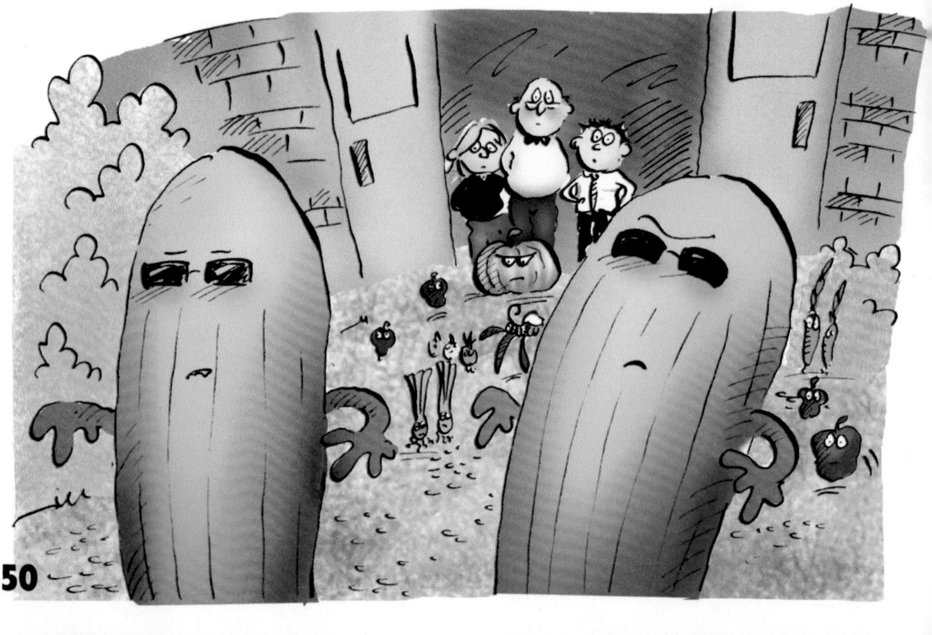

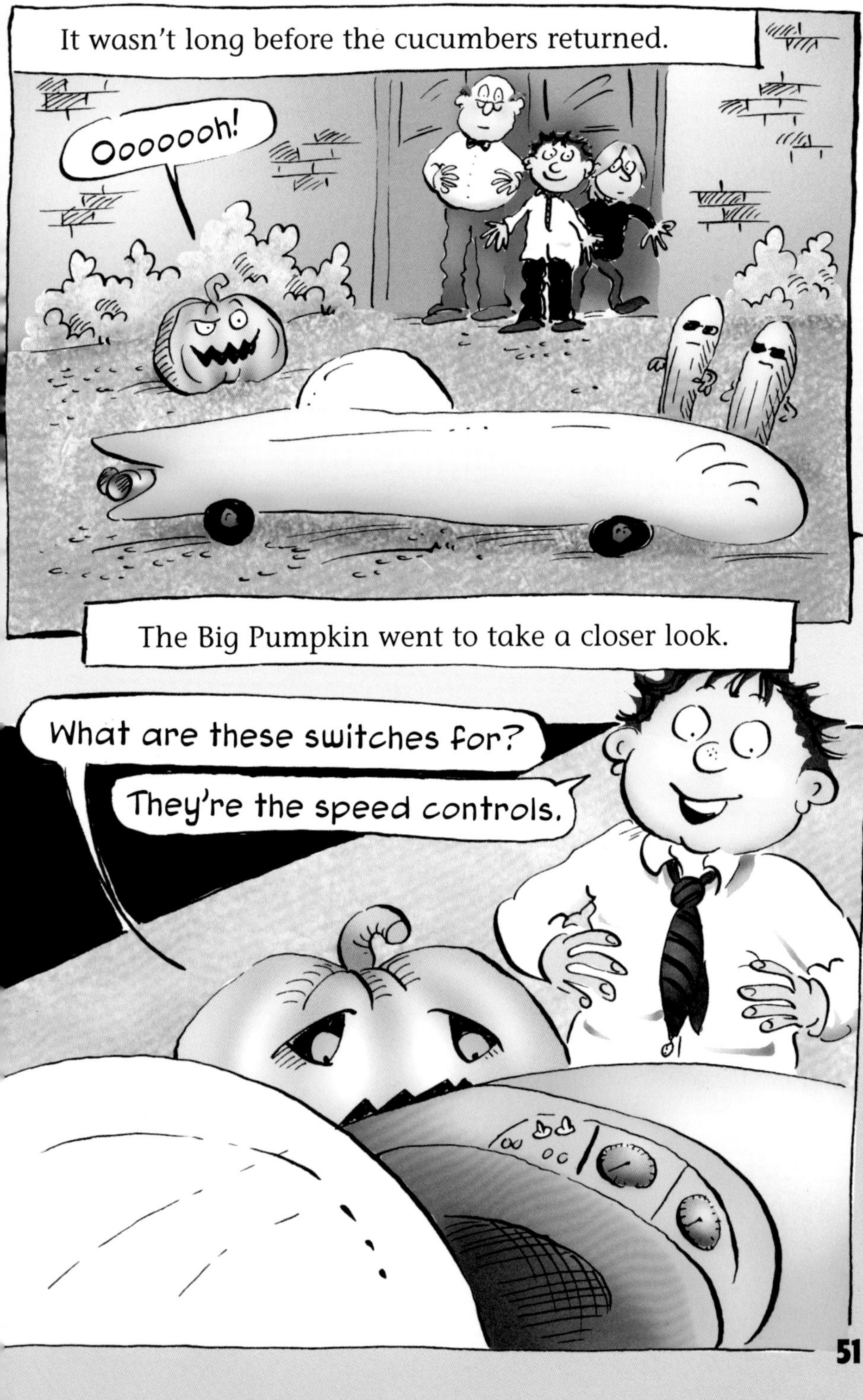
It wasn't long before the cucumbers returned.
Ooooooh!
The Big Pumpkin went to take a closer look.
What are these switches for?
They're the speed controls.

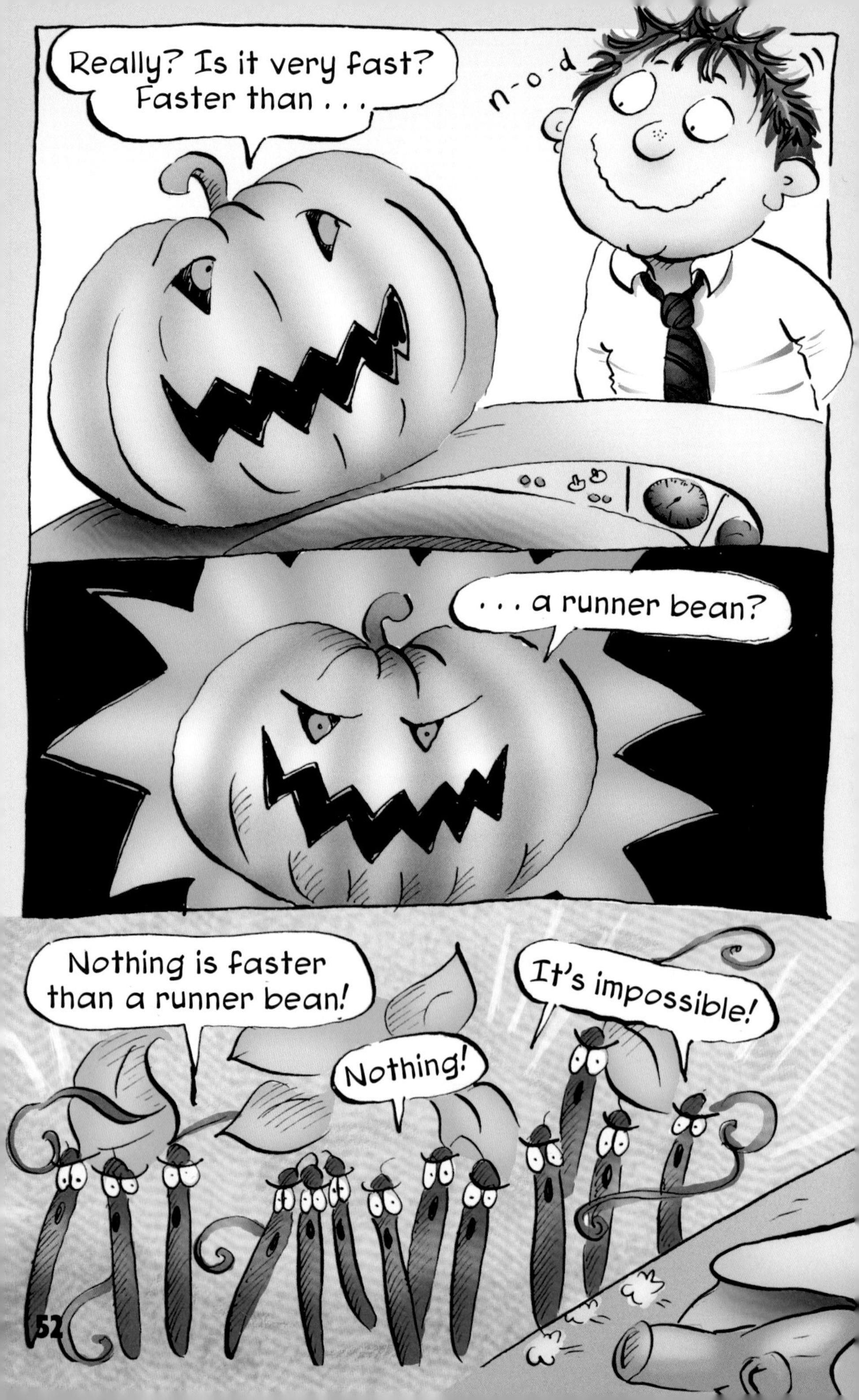
Really? Is it very fast? Faster than . . .
n-o-d
. . . a runner bean?
Nothing is faster than a runner bean!
Nothing!
It's impossible!

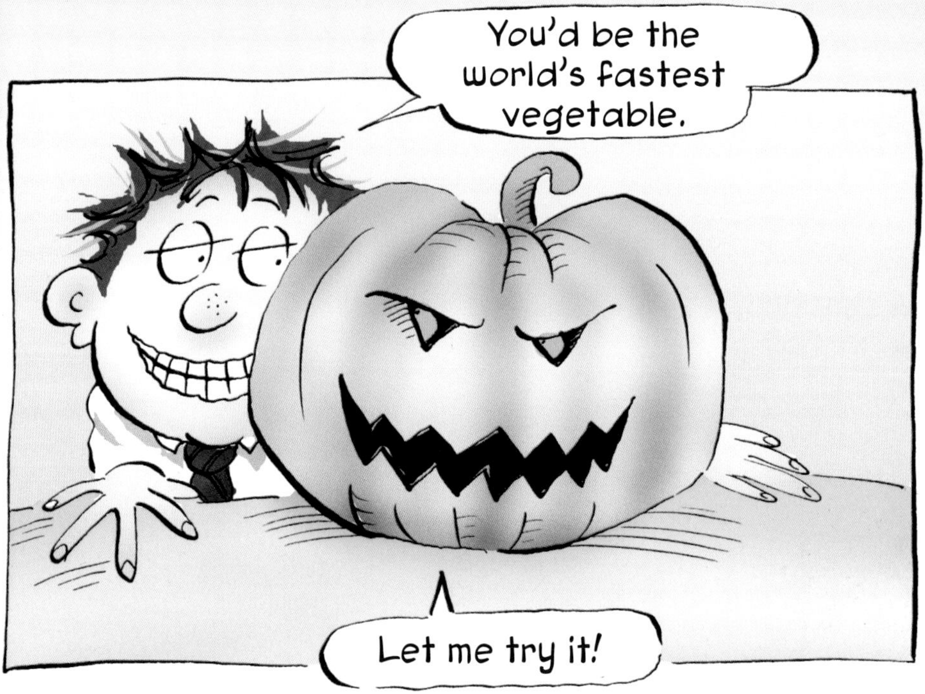
You'd be the world's fastest vegetable.
Let me try it!

The Big Pumpkin got into the race car and pressed the controls.

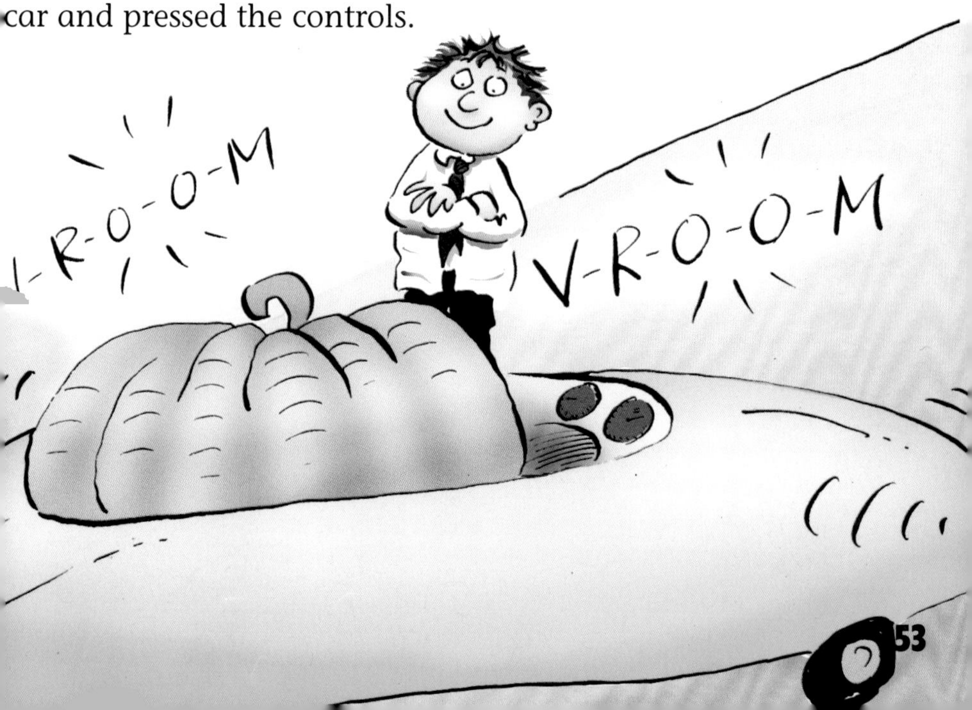
R-O-O-M
V-R-O-O-M

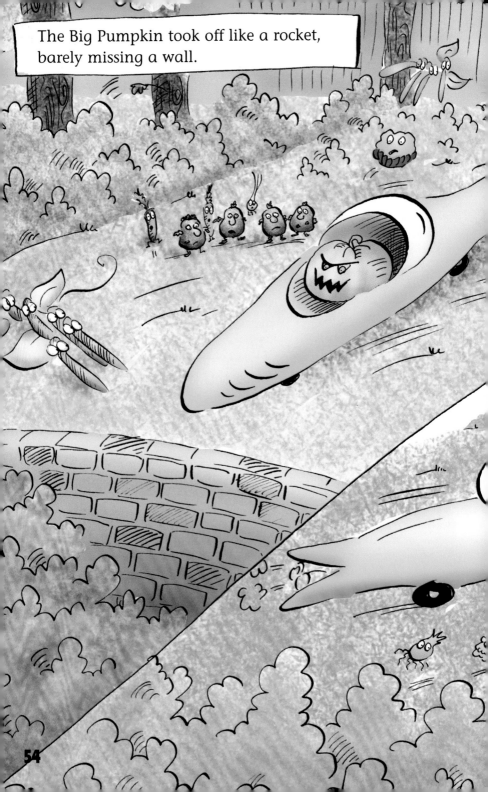

The Big Pumpkin took off like a rocket, barely missing a wall.

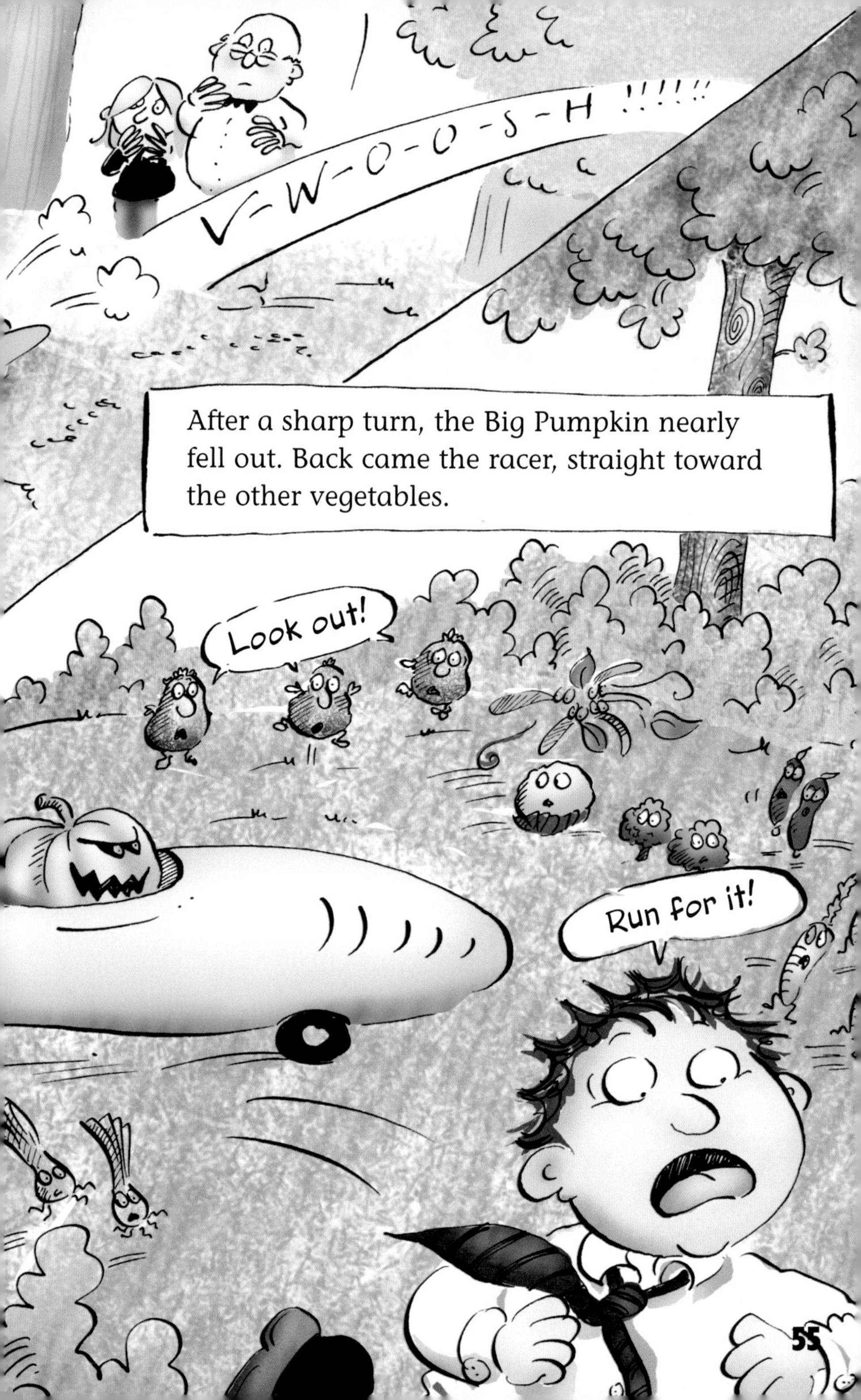
V-W-O-O-S-H!!!!!!
After a sharp turn, the Big Pumpkin nearly fell out. Back came the racer, straight toward the other vegetables.
Look out!
Run for it!

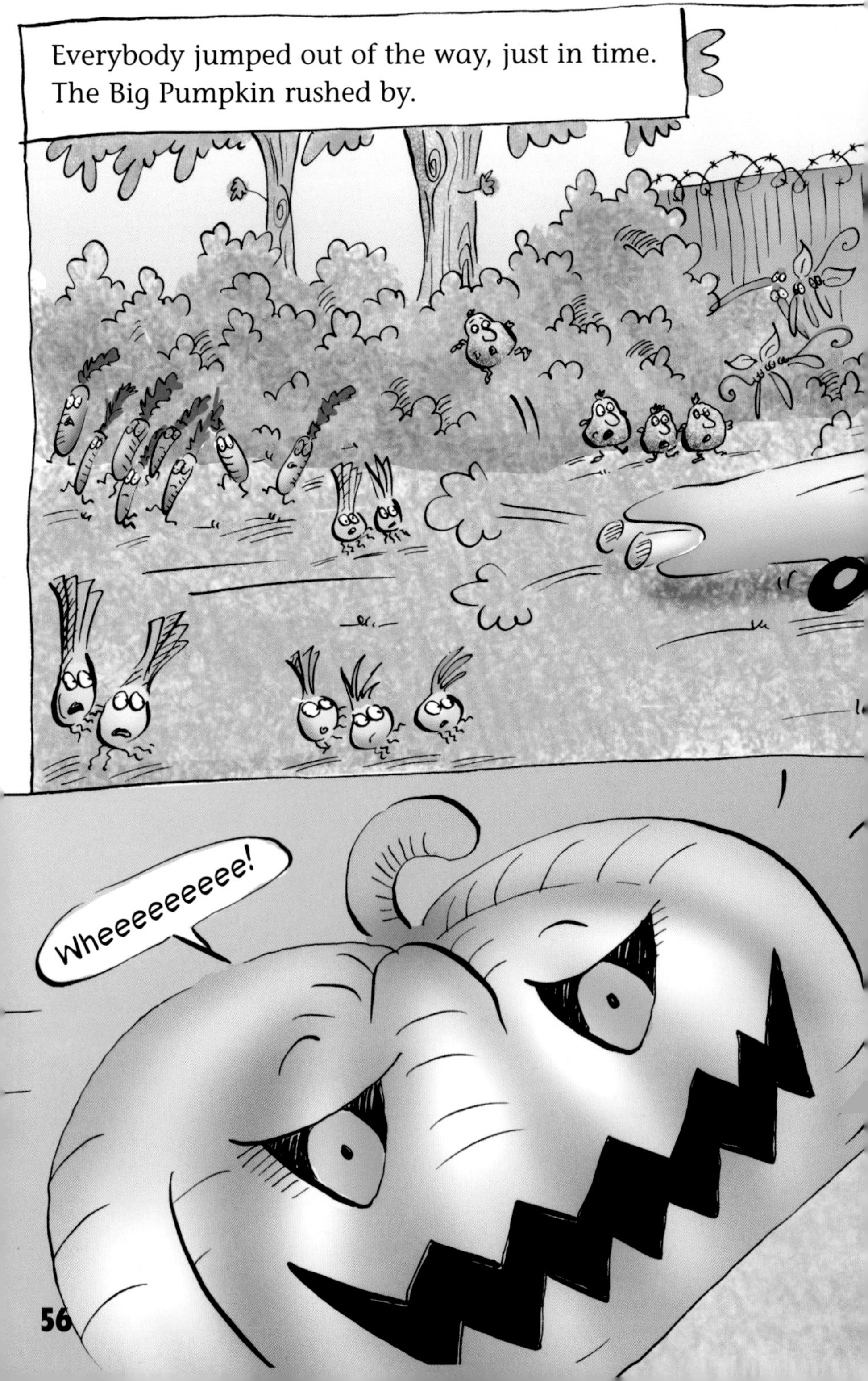
Everybody jumped out of the way, just in time.
The Big Pumpkin rushed by.
Wheeeeeeeee!

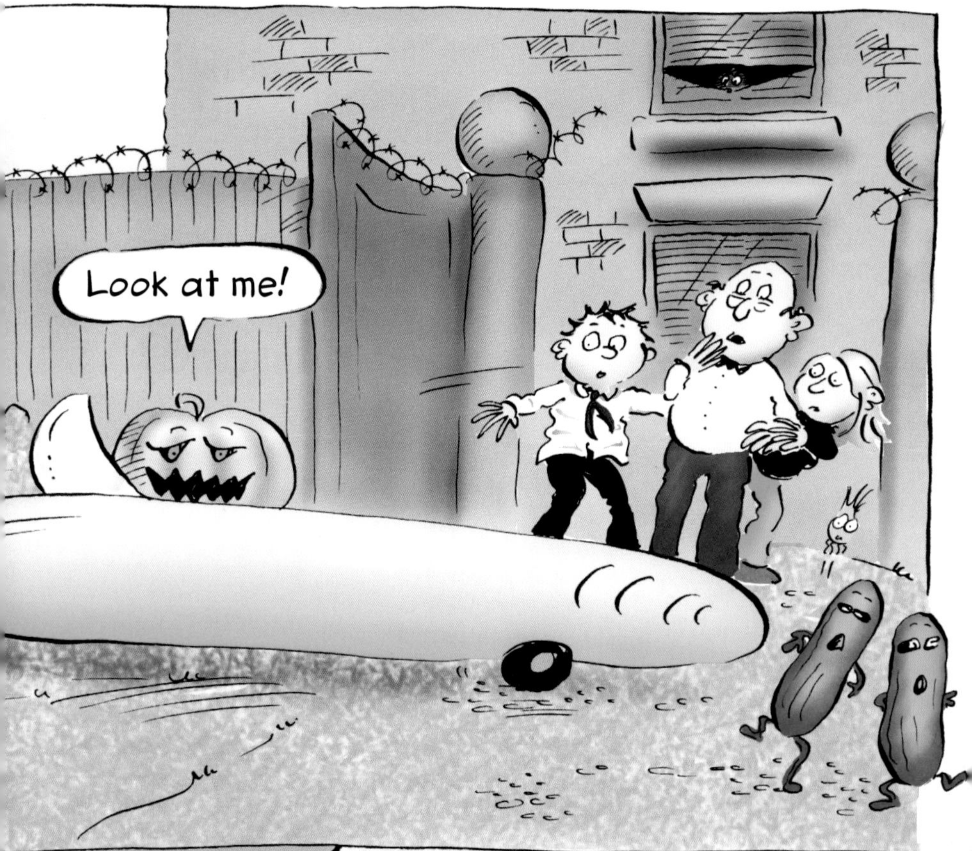
Look at me!

The car headed for the compost bin. Spike shouted a command.

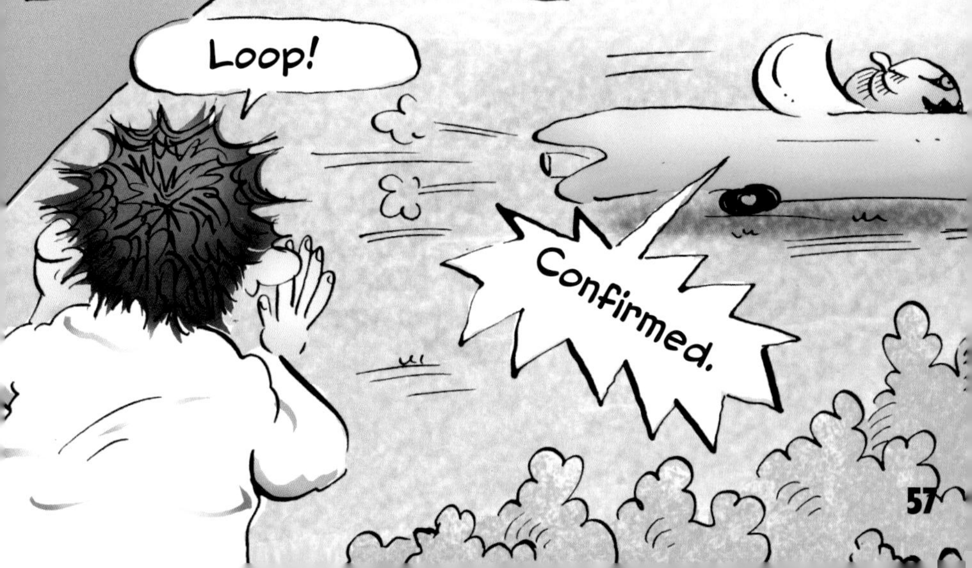
Loop!
Confirmed.

Suddenly, the car spun around. Taken by surprise, the Big Pumpkin lost control and flipped out.

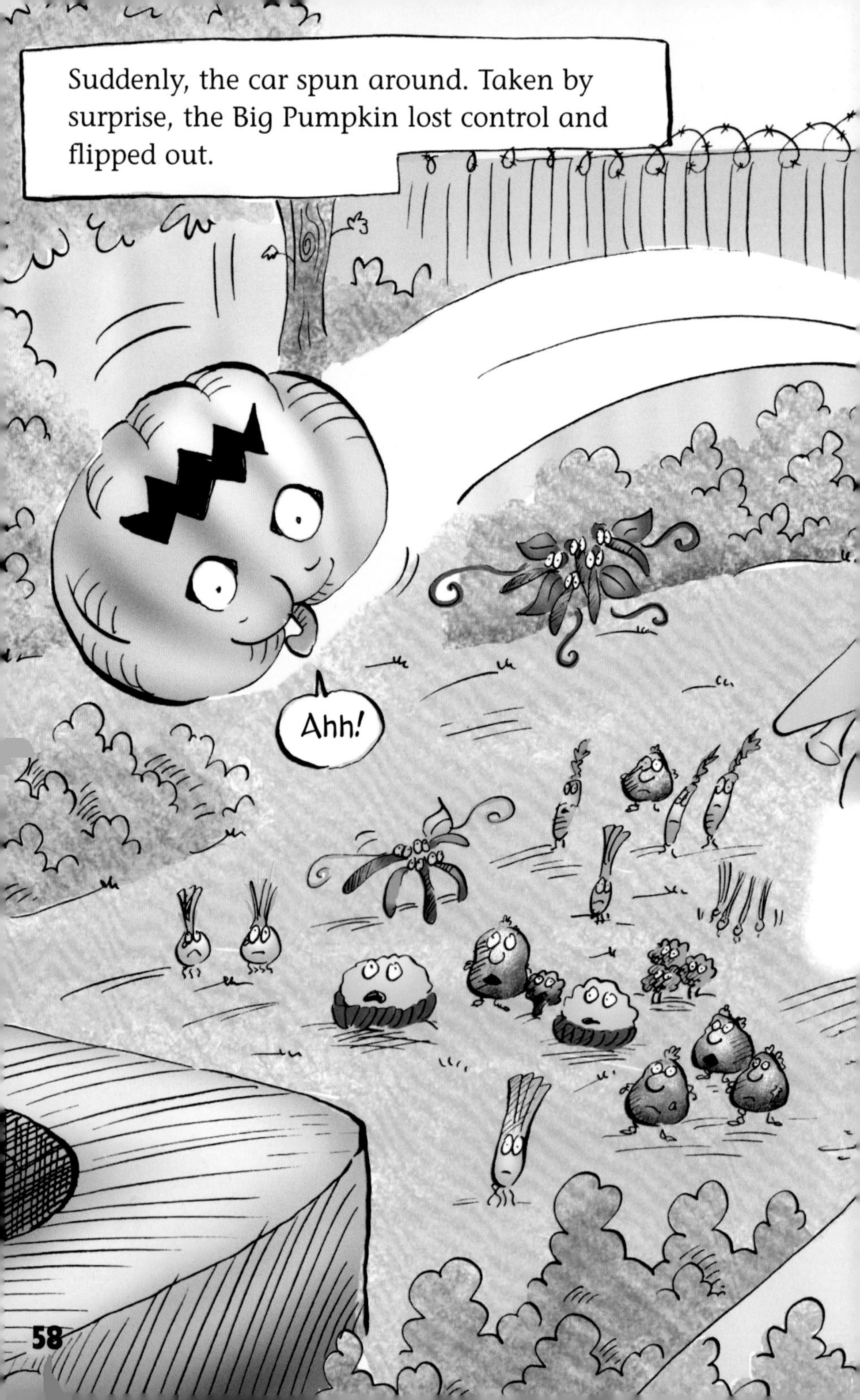
Ahh!

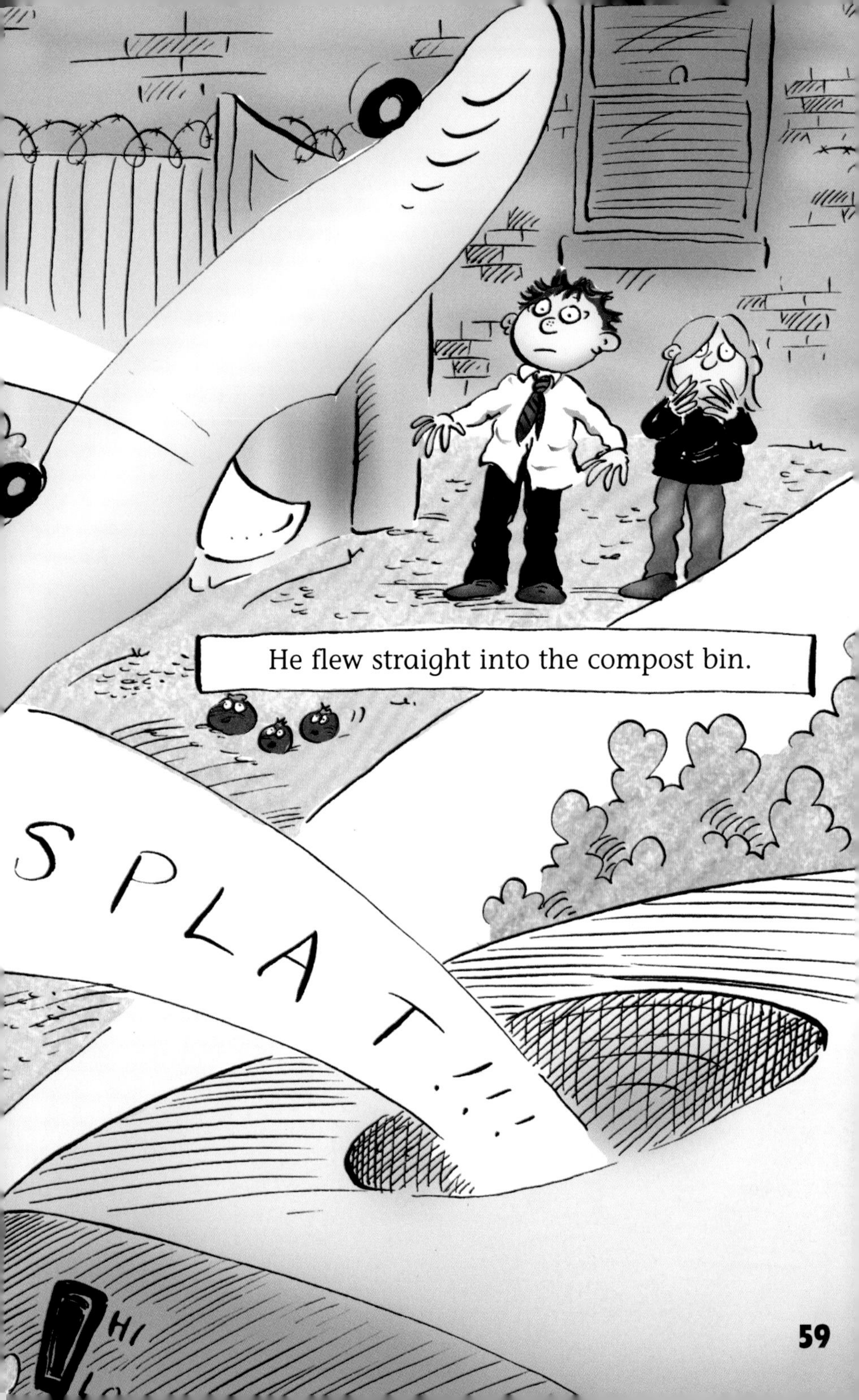
He flew straight into the compost bin.
SPLAT!

Chapter Eight

The vegetables were horrified that the Big Pumpkin had been destroyed. They ran around afraid, completely lost without their leader.

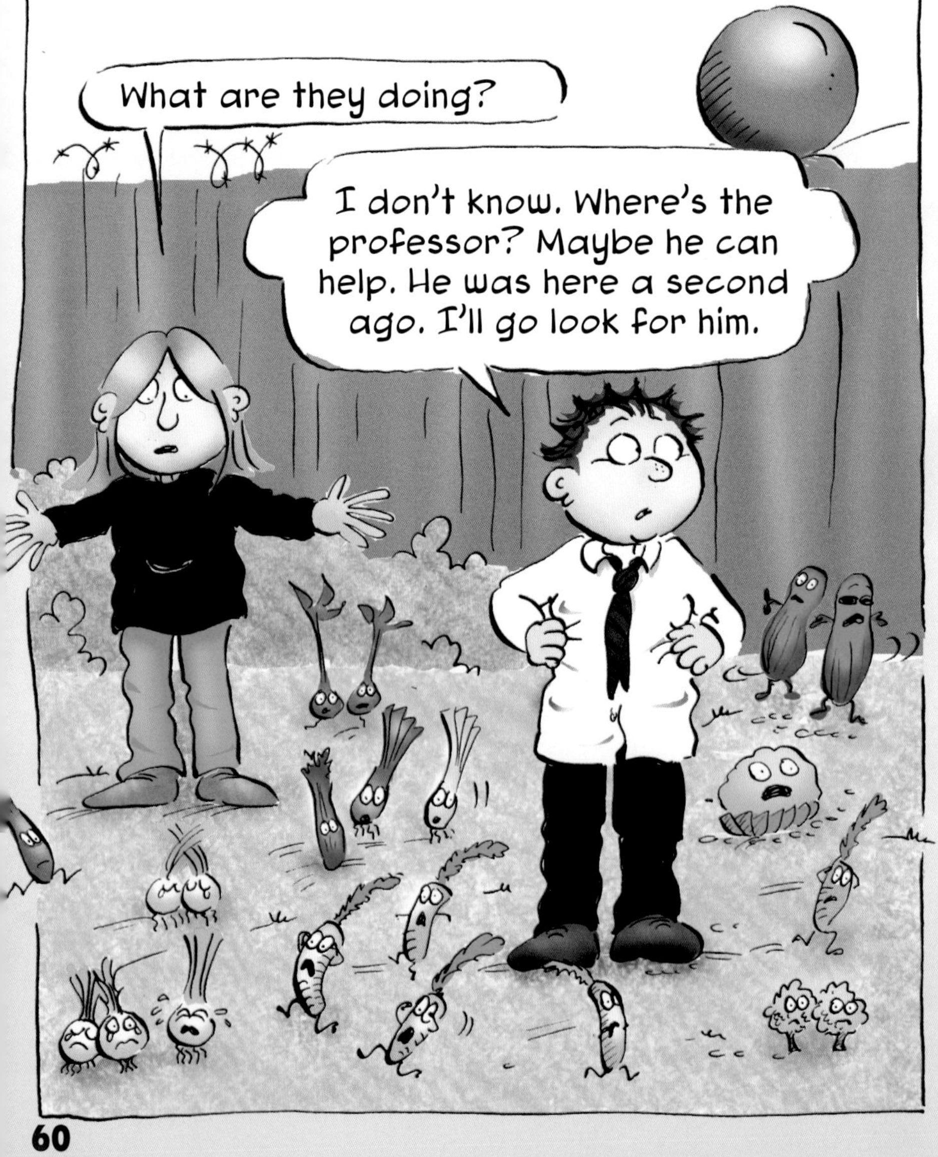
What are they doing?
I don't know. Where's the professor? Maybe he can help. He was here a second ago. I'll go look for him.

Then suddenly, the professor appeared, followed by the Project X tomatoes. The friendly tomatoes ran to talk to the other vegetables.

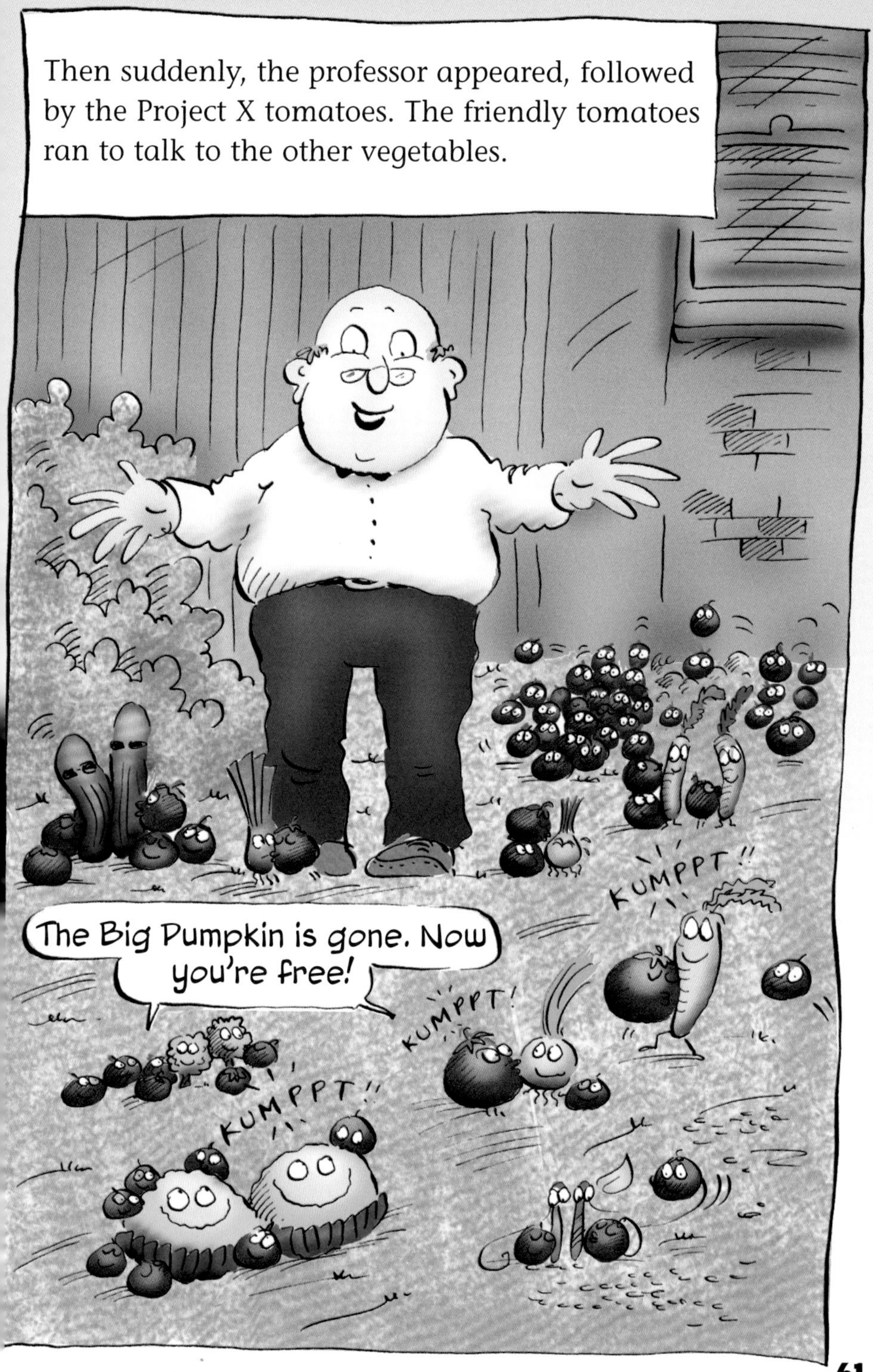
The Big Pumpkin is gone. Now you're free!
KUMPPT!!
KUMPPT!
KUMPPT!!

The vegetables finally calmed down.

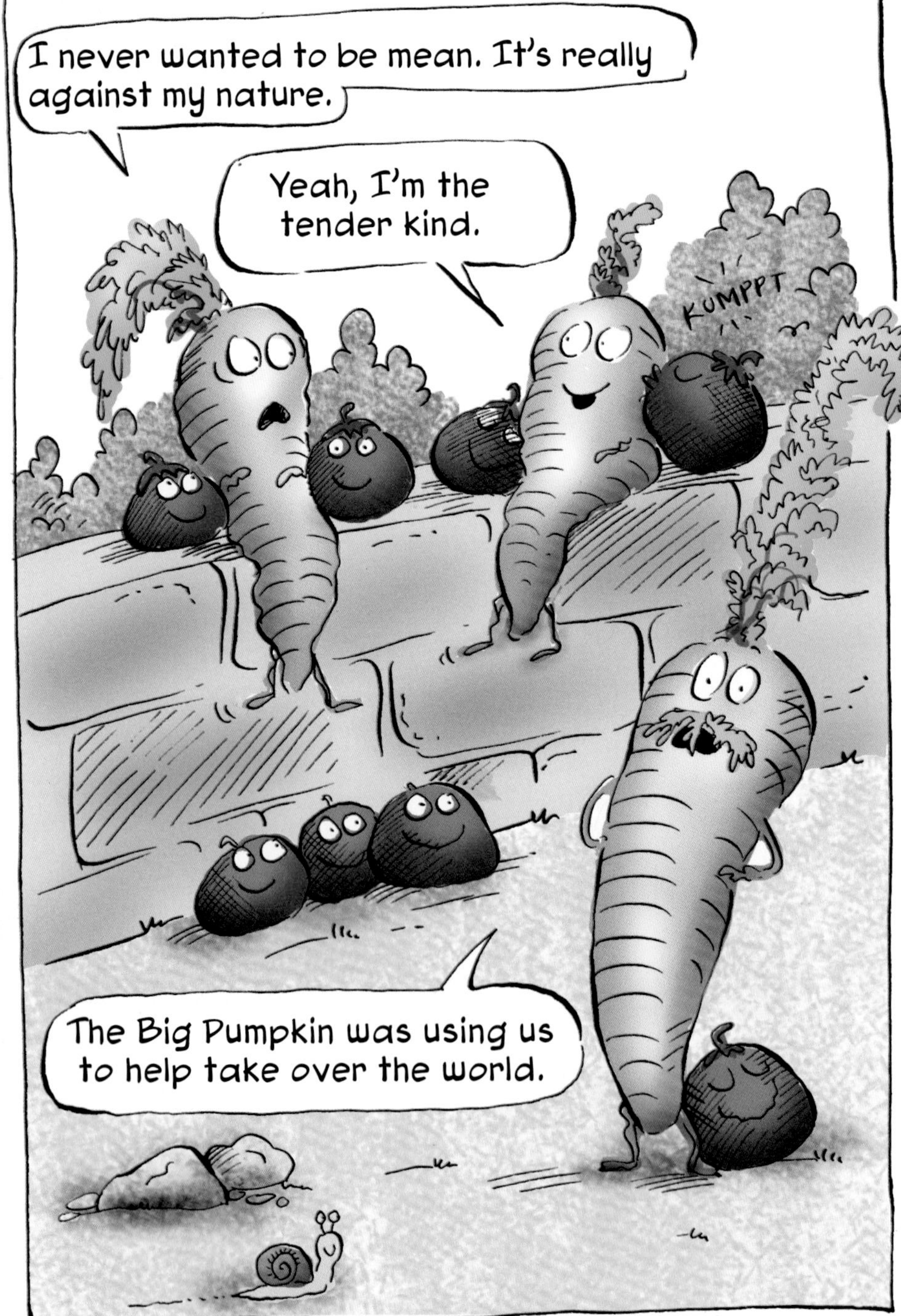

I never wanted to be mean. It's really against my nature.
Yeah, I'm the tender kind.
KUMPPT
The Big Pumpkin was using us to help take over the world.

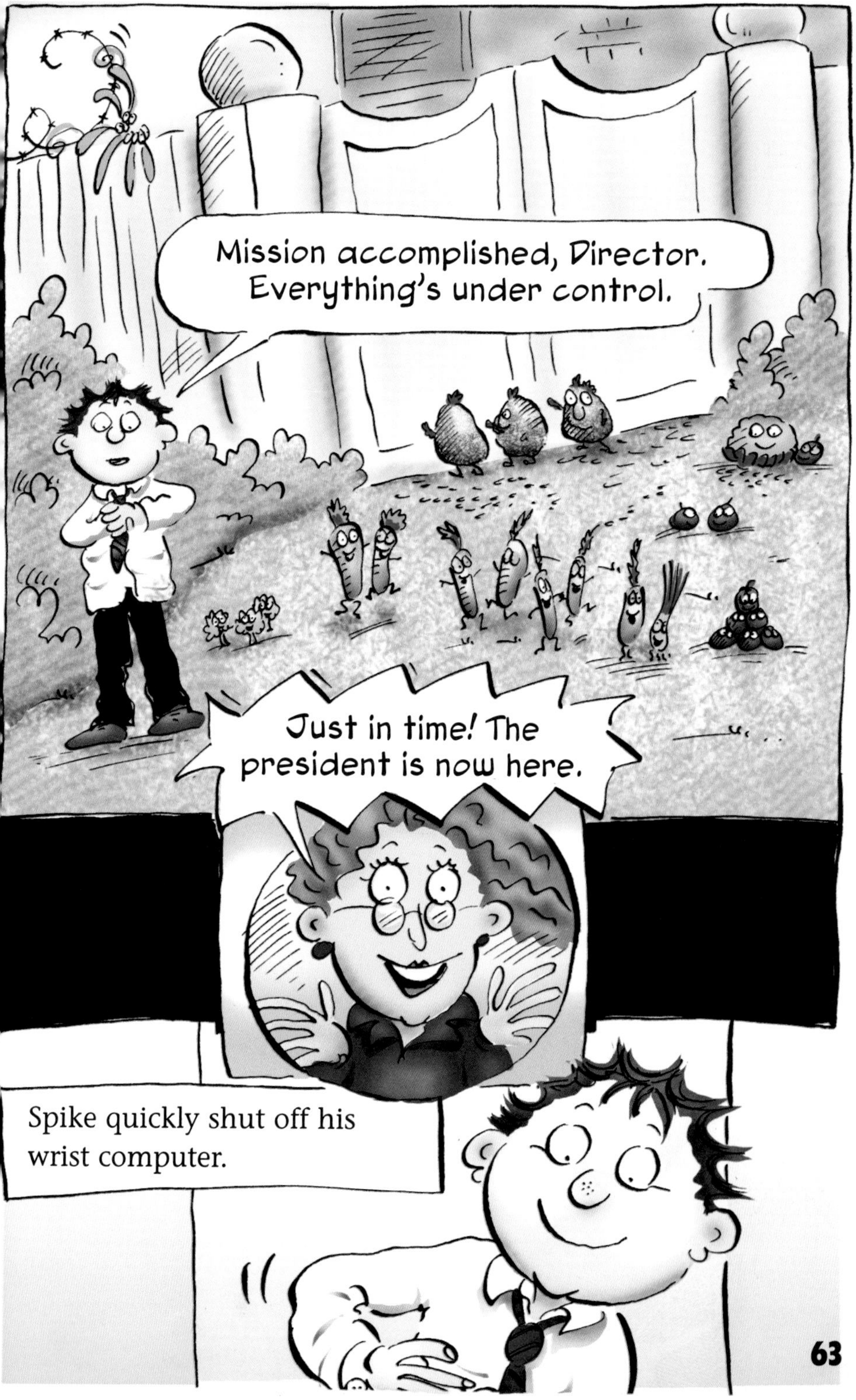
Mission accomplished, Director. Everything's under control.
Just in time! The president is now here.
Spike quickly shut off his wrist computer.

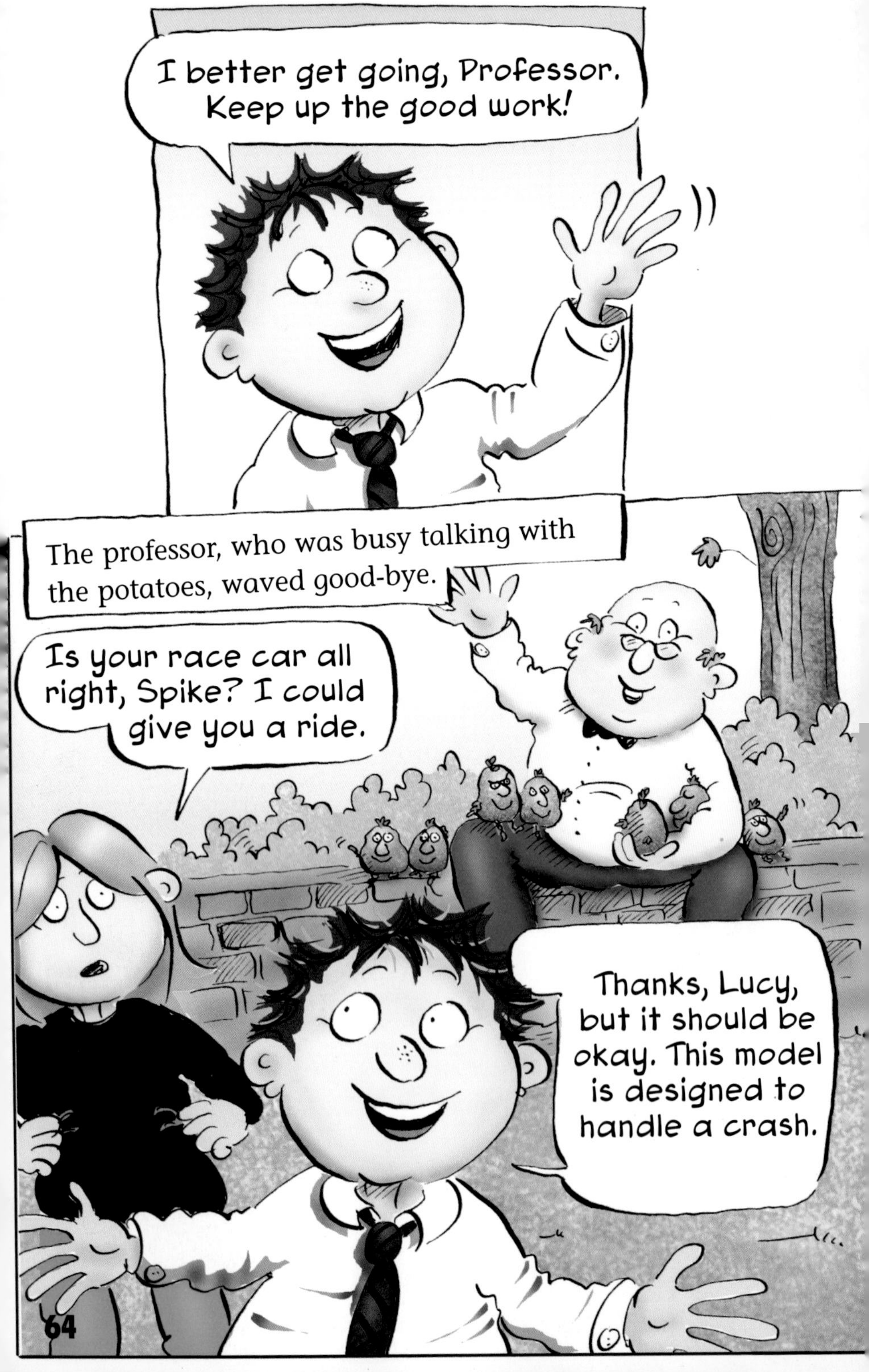
I better get going, Professor. Keep up the good work!
The professor, who was busy talking with the potatoes, waved good-bye.
Is your race car all right, Spike? I could give you a ride.
Thanks, Lucy, but it should be okay. This model is designed to handle a crash.

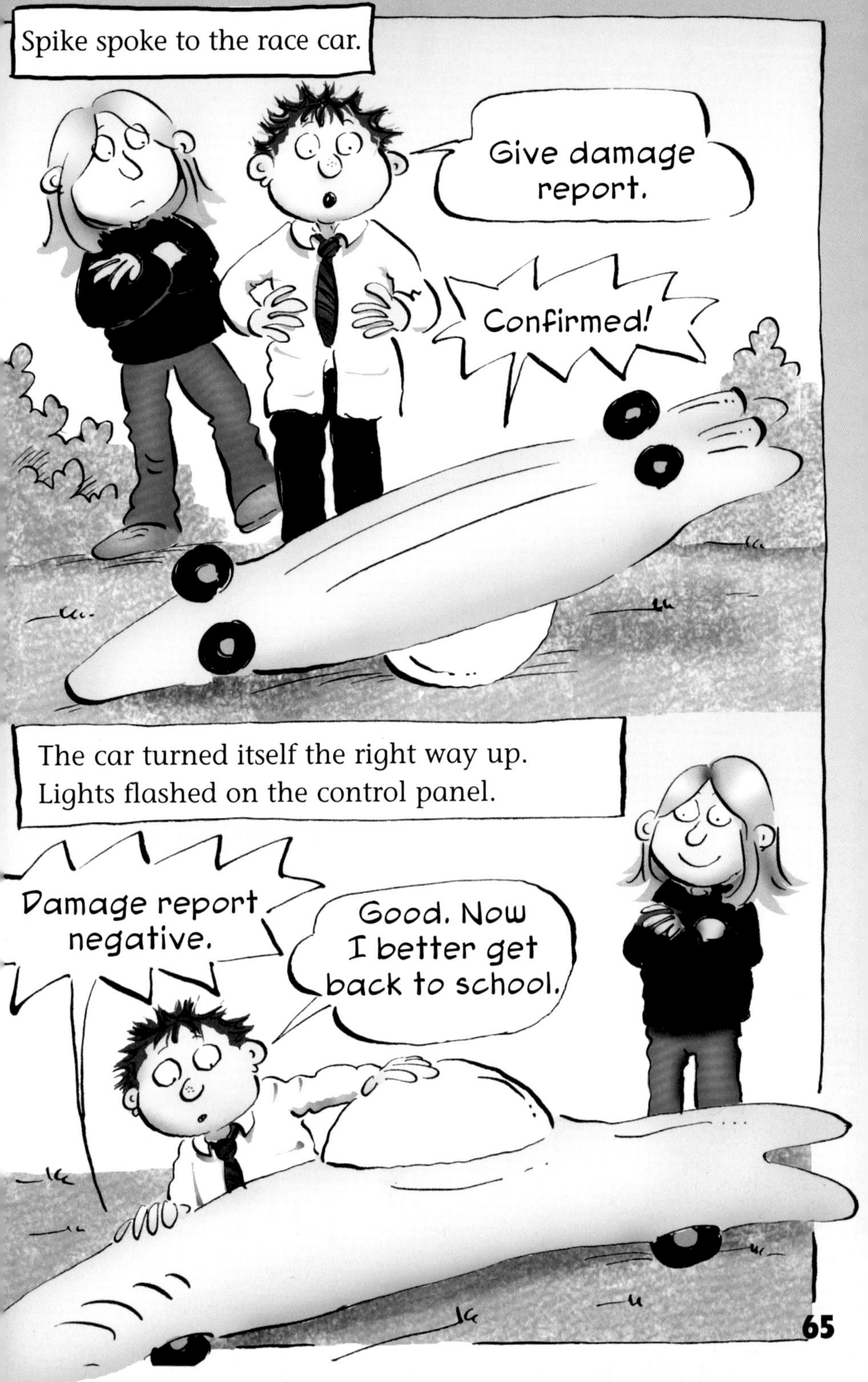
Spike spoke to the race car.
Give damage report.
Confirmed!
The car turned itself the right way up. Lights flashed on the control panel.
Damage report negative.
Good. Now I better get back to school.

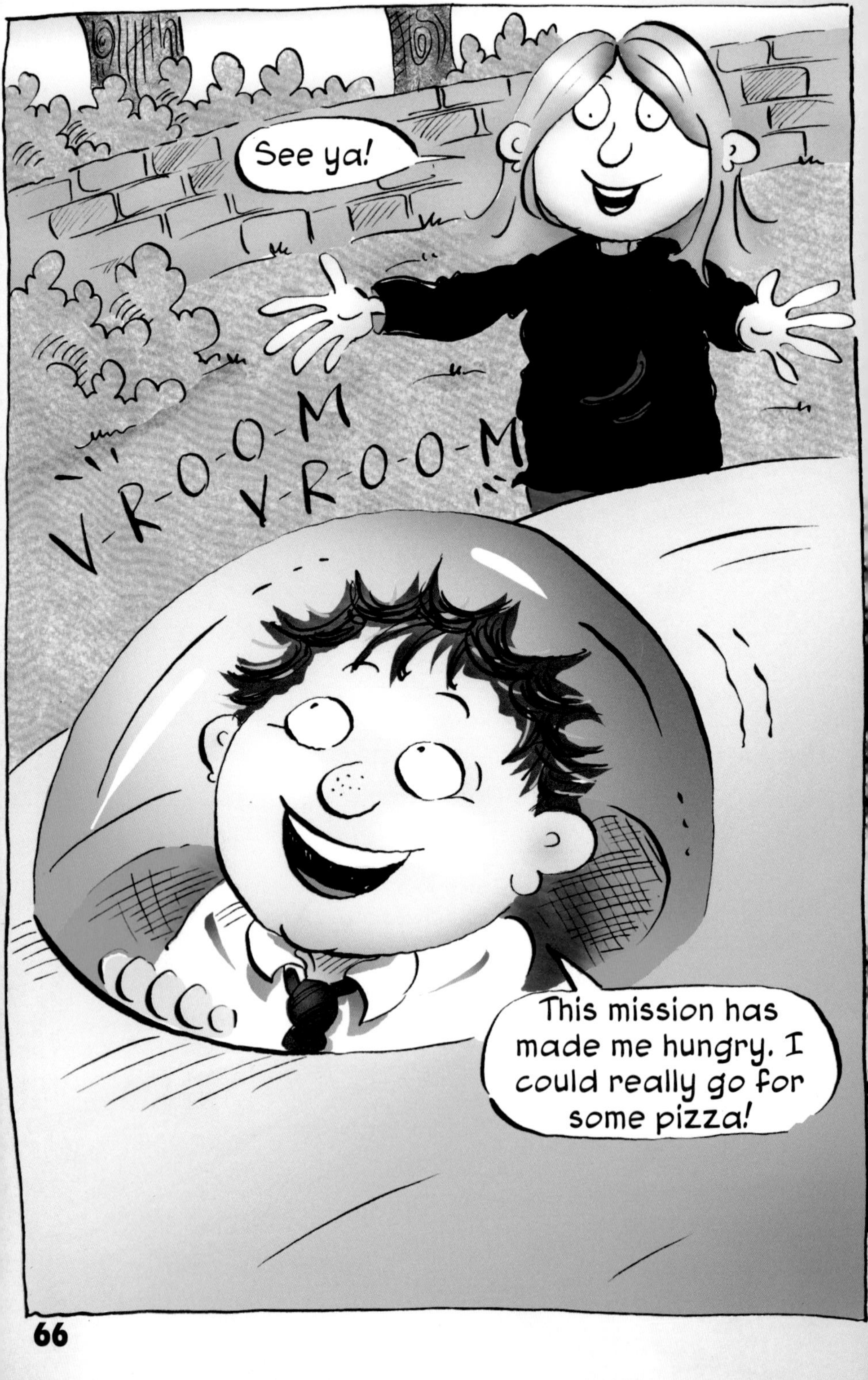
See ya!
V-R-O-O-M V-R-O-O-M
This mission has made me hungry. I could really go for some pizza!

ABOUT THE AUTHOR

Mark Burgess lives in England with his wife and cat. During the past 25 years, he has written and illustrated more than 60 children's books, with plenty more to come. When he's not writing or painting, he spends time in his vegetable garden. So far, he says, all is quiet between the beans and tomatoes.

ABOUT THE ILLUSTRATOR

Bridget MacKeith lives in a tiny English village with her husband, two children, and her big, hairy dog, Rudi. MacKeith enjoys mountain biking, running, swimming, and other outdoor activities. More than anything, though, she loves to draw. "I'm lucky that my work is a favorite pastime, so it almost passes as a hobby," she says. MacKeith has worked on many children's books and also illustrates greeting cards for Hallmark.

GLOSSARY

command (kuh-MAND)—an order or request

compost (KOM-pohst)—a mixture of rotting leaves, weeds, and vegetables that farmers add to soil to help crops grow

compost bin (KOM-pohst BIN)—the container where compost is made

hostages (HOSS-tih-jez)—people taken prisoner by another person or group

mission (MISH-uhn)—an important task or job

morph (MORF)—to transform or change shape

plot (PLOT)—a secret and often evil plan

resistance (ri-ZISS-tuhnss)—trying to fight back against someone or something

runner bean (RUH-nuhr BEEN)—a type of bean from Central America with red flowers; also known as the **scarlet runner bean**

urgent (UR-juhnt)—needing immediate attention

INTERNET SITES

Do you want to know more about subjects related to this book? Or are you interested in learning about other topics? Then check out FactHound, a fun, easy way to find Internet sites.

Our investigative staff has already sniffed out great sites for you!

Here's how to use FactHound:

1. Visit *www.facthound.com*

2. Select your grade level.

3. To learn more about subjects related to this book, type in the book's ISBN number: **9781434204585**.

4. Click the **Fetch It** button.

FactHound will fetch the best Internet sites for you.

DISCUSSION QUESTIONS

1. The Big Pumpkin was really mean. So why do you think all of the other vegetables followed him? Have you ever followed along with someone even though you knew it was wrong? Explain your answers.

2. If vegetables really did come alive, what veggie would you be the most afraid of? Why?

3. Do you think Agent Spike could have stopped the vegetables alone? Describe some of the ways other people or vegetables helped him.

WRITING PROMPTS

1. In this story, vegetables come alive and start taking over the world. Write a story about something else coming alive, such as fruits, machines, or trees. How would you stop them?

2. This book told the story of one day in the life of Agent Spike. Write a story about another day and another adventure in his life.

3. Graphic novels, like this book, are often written and illustrated by two different people. Write your own graphic novel. Then, give your story to someone else to illustrate.

ALSO PUBLISHED BY STONE ARCH BOOKS

SPACE COPS
by Steve Bowkett
illustrated by Liz McIntosh
GRAPHIC NOVEL
STONE ARCH Adventure

Space Cops
by Steve Bowkett

While chasing the Quicksilver Gang, the Space Cops see something strange on their radar screen. It's a machine, and it's bigger than a planet! When the Space Cops investigate, they discover that the universe's most evil leader is at the controls. Can they stop him from using the planet machine to destroy Earth?

ORDER NOW!

STONE ARCH BOOKS,
151 Good Counsel Hill Drive, Mankato, MN 56001
1-800-421-7731
www.stonearchbooks.com